About
the
Sleeping
Beauty

About the Sleeping Beauty

by P.L. TRAVERS

illustrated by Charles Keeping

McGRAW-HILL BOOK COMPANY
New York   St. Louis   San Francisco   Düsseldorf
Mexico   Panama   Toronto

Library of Congress Cataloging in Publication Data

Travers, Pamela L.
  About the Sleeping Beauty.

  SUMMARY: Five versions of the sleeping beauty tale
are accompanied by the author's own version and an essay
on the meaning of fairy tales, "The Sleeping Beauty" in
particular.
    1. Fairy tales.   1. Fairy tales.   2. Folklore
I. Title.
PZ8.T724Ab   398.2'1   75-12893
ISBN 0-07-065123-X
ISBN 0-07-065122-1 lib. bdg.

Book design by Sallie Baldwin

Text copyright © 1975 by P. L. Travers
Illustrations copyright © 1975 by Charles Keeping

123456789RABP798765

OTHER BOOKS BY P. L. TRAVERS

Mary Poppins
Mary Poppins Comes Back
Mary Poppins Opens the Door
Mary Poppins in the Park
I Go by Sea, I Go by Land
The Fox at the Manger
Friend Monkey

Contents

Part One

The Sleeping Beauty

Once upon a time, a time that never was and is always, there lived in Arabia a sultan and his wife. They were, as sovereigns go, reasonably benevolent and as much loved by their subjects as is possible for fallible human beings. The life they led was comfortable, even, one might say, luxurious. They had spacious divans to sleep on, garments of finest silk and damask, expensive jewels to deck their persons, well-groomed horses and hounds for hunting, and for dwelling place a lordly palace in whose cellars stood numerous sacks of gold. They were well-served by their servants, well-fed by their cooks, and well-protected by their soldiers.

"Dear me," you will be saying, "some people have all the good fortune!"

But the Sultan and his wife would not, I think, have agreed with you. For this elegant life of theirs lacked one important thing.

3

Each day they looked at each other and sighed. "How lonely we are!" they told each other. "Our footsteps ring on the marble floors but who hears the echo and runs to meet us? Each season the flowers bloom anew but to whom can we say 'Now, pick them gently!'? Where is the one who will listen and gaze when we point to the stars and say 'That is Orion!'? Who will walk with us under the palm trees or count the newborn lambs on the hill? To whom shall we tell the evening tales that are running in our minds? There is no one to be our care while we live and to weep for us when we die. If only we had a child!"

And then, since a man cannot grieve continually— though the same thing is not true of women—the Sultan would go about his work, ordering the affairs of his country. Or he would clap his hands for his dark slave, Bouraba, and send him with letters or ultimatums to the rulers of the surrounding kingdoms. In such ways, by keeping himself well-occupied, he was able to forget for a while the heaviness in his heart.

But the Sultana did not forget for a moment. Women brood over their troubles as hens brood upon eggs. Day after day she would sit under a wild rose tree by the lake and fold her arms and rock her sorrow as though it were a wakeful child. But it never went to sleep.

One day as she sat there, a frog sprang straight up out of the lake and landed on a stone beside her. His neck pulsed in and out with his breath, and his eyes, reflecting the glint of the dark water, regarded her thoughtfully.

"Why do you grieve, Sultana, rocking backwards and forwards? Morning after morning the same scene spreads before me—a great lady, who should have something better

4

to do, weeping and swaying to and fro, wasting her life away. Tell me, why is this?"

So the Sultana told him.

"Here," she said, touching her belly. "And here," she said, touching her breast. "And here," she said, touching the inner crease of her elbow, "I ache for what I lack."

On and on she went with her story, relating it in the mournful voice that she and the Sultan together used in their nightly tale of woe.

"Dear me," said the frog, "how very sad! But wait a little while, Sultana. I promise you that in less than a year you will have your lack no longer."

The Sultana stared. "How can you know that?" she protested, with a shade of irritation. For the truth was that all unknown to herself she had become so fond of her sorrow that now the mere thought of losing it made her feel naked and bereft. "After all, you are only a frog."

"Only a frog," the frog agreed. "As you are only a woman."

"On the other hand," the Sultana mused, following her own train of thought. "There is an old story of a prince who turned into a frog. And it may be, since you speak with sagacity, that you, perhaps, are he."

"Ah, so I must be human to be wise—is that what you think? Well, the sun rises promptly every morning, rivers flow downhill rather than up, the seed breaks the pod when the time is ripe. Were these taught their changeless ways by man? Dear madam, if I were that prince—and, mind you, I am not admitting it!—I would beg whatever magician changed me to let me remain a frog. A man sees no further than his nose. So, for that matter, does a frog. On the other hand, a frog lives in water, down by the roots, and senses what is stirring. And this frog bids you dry your eyes. Go home now, Sultana, and come no more to the wild rose tree. The time for that is past."

With that, the frog unceremoniously turned his back and snatched at a passing fly.

The Sultana stood gazing at him in wonder. "Life is full of surprises," she murmured at last. Then she turned and went thoughtfully back to the palace.

That evening she surprised her husband by saying "Let us not grieve at all tonight. It may be that grief has become a habit and that only by asking nothing can any wish come true. Let us walk among the flowers simply for our own delight and gaze up at the stars for the same reason."

So they did that, with great pleasure. And eventually, in a year—all but three months—the frog's prophecy was fulfilled and a daughter was born.

The Sultan received the news with satisfaction tempered with disappointment. "I could have asked for nothing better, except, of course, a son."

But the Sultana, holding her baby in her arms, was utterly content. She had no ache anywhere and she felt that she lacked nothing.

"When you are given a lily," she advised her husband, "do not protest that it should have been a tulip."

"Nevertheless," replied the Sultan, "we need a successor to the throne and a son would have been very useful."

At that, as though she felt herself to be unwelcome, the baby set up a doleful weeping and the Sultan, a good-hearted man in spite of a certain irritability of temper, hurried to make amends.

"There, there!" He patted the wailing bundle. "I was

simply speaking my thoughts aloud and thinking about the kingdom. There's really no reason to be upset. You have almost fulfilled my dearest wish. Having waited so many years, I'm glad to get anything, truly I am, especially—" he touched her cheek. "Especially someone so pretty."

No baby can resist flattery, so the Princess, drinking back her tears, smiled and contentedly fell asleep. And the Sultan hurried to the Council Chamber to tell the Vizier the happy news.

And the Vizier told the seneschal, who told the courtiers, who told the handmaidens, who told the pages, who told the upper servants, who told the lower servants, who told the swineherds, who told the swine. And the whole palace rejoiced.

Messengers rode to all points of the compass, proclaiming the news to the people. Bells were rung for three days and nights without ceasing, no matter whose sleep was disturbed. And every person in the land was given a piece of silver.

The next thing to be thought of was the christening.

"Bid the cooks," said the Sultan, "prepare a feast. We cannot let an event of this kind pass without a celebration. Invitations must go to all my kinsmen, friends, and acquaintances, lords and ladies. And lastly, but by no means least, we must send for the Wise Women. Those ladies lend an air of elegance to any entertainment. Apart from that, one should always keep, as it were, on the right side of them, for they have in their power the bestowal of desirable attributes and gifts of surpassing value. As a matter of policy, as well as courtesy, I wish them to be well-disposed towards my daughter. But, now that I come to think of it, a problem arises here."

The Sultan thoughtfully stroked his beard.

"There are thirteen Wise Women in the kingdom. Unfortunately, however, I have only twelve gold plates. What is to be done? I cannot insult any single fairy by giving her a china dish while her sisters eat off gold. One of them, therefore, must stay at home. But which one? What a quandary!"

He pondered the question for a moment. Then he clapped his hands.

"Bouraba!" he cried. And the dark slave fell to his knees before him.

"Bouraba, you shall be my courier. Take these twelve invitations and present one, with my compliments, to each of the first twelve fairies who happen to cross your path. And now," he said to the Sultana, as Bouraba bowed himself away, "we must wait and hope for the best."

How far is it to fairyland? Nearer by far than Babylon. It intersects our mortal world at every point and at every second. The two of them together make one web woven fine. It was no time, therefore, before Bouraba had performed his task and was back again at the palace.

The Wise Women, for people who believe in them, are never far to seek. Wherever a cradle is set rocking, the hand of some Wise Woman lies over the mortal hand. Wherever mother and daughter are, talking the age-old talk of women, a Wise Woman makes a third. They mix with the matrons at the market, the fishwives by the harbour's edge, and ladies in elegant mansions; they nod with the grandmothers by the fire; they dance with the demoiselles at the crossroads. When a young child laughs all alone, be sure he has seen a Wise Woman pass; when an old man weeps all alone, he has surely seen the same thing and is grieving for his wasted days. There is no corner of existence that has not felt the Wise Women's prodding fingers. They mourn with the mourner, rejoice with the joyous. They rain down fortune on those who listen to their advice; but he who defies them, offends or neglects them, oh, let him beware! For him they are furies, probing his vitals, tempting him to his own destruction or thrusting him into misfortune's arms.

It was fortunate for Bouraba that he was a simple man of sound instinct and good feeling and was thus able to approach them with proper awe and deference. Having delivered his invitations, he left behind him twelve Wise Women well satisfied with his demeanour and the Sultan's courtesy. Enjoying, as they have ever done, all forms of festival and ceremony, they looked forward to the christening of the Princess Rose with the happiest anticipation.

At last the great day—as must happen, even with small days—arrived. Everyone in the palace, from the Sultan down to the kitchen boys, had new clothes for the occasion. The guests arrived in a glittering throng, lords and viziers on horseback, the ladies carried in palanquins. And the shining palace outshone the stars as the Sultan and Sultana led the way to the Council Chamber where beside the throne, rocked in her cradle by Bouraba, the little Princess lay.

Then, kneeling or bowing, according to their social stations, the guests proffered their gifts. These were received by the Vizier who, salaaming, handed them to the Sultan, who handed them to the Treasurer, who carried them away.

Bright-liveried servants, like butterflies, flitted among the guests, offering trays of date-palm wine and sherbet cooled by snow from the mountains. The music of lute and flute was echoed by the tinkle of talk and laughter. Everyone was as gay as the sky is blue and the courtly merriment was at its height when a sudden peal of bells rang out and silenced every voice. Nobody spoke in the Council Chamber as the twelve fairies swept in.

Not a sound did the Wise Women make as their bare feet of gold or silver floated, as is customary in the fairy world, some inches above the floor. The twelve figures seemed to hang in the air, their naked golden and silver heads gleaming above the swirling robes which were every colour of the rainbow.

In silence everybody bowed. Then the Sultan stepped forward with open arms.

"Welcome, dear ladies," he cried, salaaming, as the luminous shapes streamed across the room.

Gravely they acknowledged his greeting. Then each one, as she passed Bouraba, favoured him with a stately nod and accepted from his outstretched hand a gold plate piled with sweetmeats. They daintily picked at the mortal food and, floating away to the Princess's cradle, hovered there in a brilliant cluster, their bare heads bent above it.

Silently they took stock of the child, their austere faces wordlessly communing as though together they were pondering on what fate should be hers.

At length they all raised their heads and a deeper hush fell over the hall. You could have heard a feather fall. This, as everybody knew, was the great moment of the evening, in fact, its very meaning.

The guests leaned forward, anticipating wonders, for after all, you do not have twelve Wise Women at a christening for nothing. The Sultan and Sultana modestly smiled, attempting to convey the impression that they were keenly expectant and at the same time politely unaware that there was anything to be expected.

Two red-clad fairies broke the silence and, as so often happens at christenings, they did so in verse.

> *Her beauty shall the world surprise,*

said the first.

> *Ruby lip and starry eyes.*

The Sultana smiled a gratified smile. The Sultan, too, appeared complacent.

"A useful commodity," he murmured. "It will help me to find her a husband."

Then the second, swirling in flamy robes, lifted her silver hand.

> *Health to her that shall be spun*
> *From earth and fire and wind and sun.*

"Ah," cried the guests among themselves. "Spun from all the elements. That is health indeed."

"H'mm," said the Sultan to himself. "That will save the apothecary's bills. I'm glad of health, naturally. But what of wealth, I wonder?" And he eagerly eyed two orange fairies who were joining hands across the cradle.

> *You will find in east or west*
> *No kinder heart in any breast*

declared one. And her sister added,

> *A good temper, sweet and mild,*
> *Shall I give the Sultan's child.*

The Sultan and Sultana bowed, she with happy gratitude but he, it has to be confessed, with growing irritation.

"Kind hearts are all very fine," he muttered. "But who will give her a coronet? Well, well, here are two more fairies. Let us see what they have in their pockets."

The yellow fairies, fragile as lilies, were waving silver hands.

I'll give her joy,

said the first, briefly.

Without alloy,

the other added.

"So kind, so kind," the Sultana murmured.

The Sultan nodded and shuffled his feet. It was as much as he could do not to stamp them.

It was now the turn of the green fairies. The two bent and waved, like grass in the wind, as they spoke with a single voice:

> *No bird or beast shall fear her*
> *No malice shall come near her.*

And immediately afterwards, the ninth and tenth fairies, cloudily blue as the evening sky, proclaimed their magic gifts:

> *Beneath her bed no crouching bear,*
> *No shadowy corner on the stair,*
> *Like candle in the dark she'll go,*
> *Not dreading any mortal foe.*

The Sultana responded with a smile, the Sultan with a throaty rumble, as the eleventh fairy, trailing her sea-coloured indigo robes, lifted her head from the cradle.

> *Contentment and a quiet mind,*
> *And what she looks for she shall find.*

The Sultan gave her an outraged stare. Then, suddenly remembering his manners, he made a deep, back-breaking bow, spread out his hands and shook his head like one who is at loss for words.

"Kind fairies, thank you, one and all. Such *useful* presents. They leave me speechless."

But behind his peacock feather fan, he whispered balefully to his wife. "I'm astounded! Not a penny piece! Good temper, health, peace, and joy—and not a single jewel. No bags of gold, no marble mansion. Poor child, she'll be as poor as a mouse."

The Sultana gently stroked his arm. "In the long run," she said, with a practical air, "these gifts are always the best."

"But insubstantial!" the Sultan wailed. Nothing you can touch or see. Will such gifts help to increase her dowry? No bears under the bed, they say. But who would dream of putting one there? And as for stairways, they are all well lit. She will not *need* to be a candle."

"Perhaps," said the Sultana wisely, "they meant another kind of dark."

"Nonsense! There's only one kind of dark. Well, well, never despair. We still have one gift left to get." The Sultan nodded at the Twelfth Wise Woman who was hovering at the head of the cradle, her indigo robes like waves about her. "The last gift, you know, is always the best. I am hoping for something splendid. Look, she is raising her golden hand. Allah preserve us—what is this?"

As though struck by an unseen fist, the Sultan staggered backwards. A clap of thunder rocked the hall—or was it perhaps the sound of cannon?—and a thick grey mist swept through the door. The lute strings broke with a twanging cry, the wineglasses shattered on their trays. The guests shrieked, the servants shouted, the Princess wailed.

13

"We are beseiged!" the Sultan bellowed. "Vizier, call the soldiers in! Station the guards at every point! This is a ruse of our enemies! They are now at our very gates!"

"One enemy alone, Prince, and that no mortal foe!"

A vibrant voice rang through the hall, the wreathing mist cleared away and there, standing in the air, her violet robes flowing about her, was the thirteenth of the Wise Women. Her naked silver head flashed as she turned from one point to another wrathfully eying the scene.

The Sultan's face was as pale as marble.

"Bring me my sword!" he said nervously, as the Wise Woman strode through air towards him.

She laughed mockingly.

"No sword can save you, foolish mortal! Only a word can do that. Speak it—if you can. Tell me, you little earthly lord, why all my sisters are gathered here, all invited to your daughter's christening—and I alone left out?"

Step by step she crossed the hall, thrusting the Sultan backwards.

"Well?" she demanded, ominously.

The Sultan collapsed upon the throne, rocking himself backwards and forwards, racking his brain for an answer.

"Most noble fairy, I beg forgiveness. It was not intentional, I assure you—simply a matter of dishes. Thirteen Wise Women in the land and only twelve gold plates! I should have sent an apology. But with all the christening arrangements, I was busy and I just forgot."

"Forgot!" The Wise Woman spat the word at him. "And did you also fail to remember that one thing leads to another? Every stick has two ends, Prince. You forgot! And because of that, *I* am called to remember. Because of that, I—as long as your story lives—must play the part of the Wicked Fairy. Children will turn aside at my name and

men call curses on my head. You cannot alter the law, Prince. In my world there is no forgetting. And he who forgets in your world must take the consequences."

"Yes," said the Sultan, miserably. "You must punish me as you think best. I will do whatever you wish."

"You will do nothing, mortal man. You will simply accept my gift."

The Sultan stared in astonishment. Was there to be no retribution?

"Well, that's very handsome of you," he blustered. "Letting bygones be bygones."

The Wise Woman smiled a curious smile. "Yes," she said, "what is done is done. It is no use crying over spilt milk."

As she spoke she moved towards the child, taking her place at the foot of the cradle.

The Sultan preened and stroked his beard. He could hardly contain his impatience. At last, perhaps, he would get what he hoped for.

"Now," said the Wise Woman, as she laid her hand upon the child and fixed the Sultan with her eye. "Here is the gift I give your daughter":

> *She'll have her beauty, peace and joy*
> *For fifteen years without alloy.*
> *But that's the end. A spindle dart*
> *Will pierce her finger, and your heart.*
> *Oh, red the blood and white the bed,*
> *And there's your darling daughter—DEAD!*

And with a laugh that shook the pillars of the chamber and chilled the marrow of all who heard it, she swept her violet robes about her, raised her silver hand in salute and disappeared through the ceiling.

16

With a shriek, the Sultana fled to the cradle. "Oh, my darling, my dear, my love!"

"Alas, alas!" the Sultan cried. "Such a woeful punishment for such a little slip! No, do not comfort me," he sobbed, as the twelfth fairy, swirling forward, put her hand on his shoulder.

"Good mortal," she smiled at him. "Do not grieve. I still have my gift to bestow, remember!"

"But what's the good of a gift, dear madam, if there's no princess to give it to?"

"It is true," said the Twelfth Wise Woman calmly, "that I cannot unwind my sister's spell. But there are many cards in the pack and I can alter it. So here is the gift I give your daughter. Fairies and mortals, mark it well":

For fifteen years without alloy
She shall indeed have peace and joy,
And then fall, not to death, but sleep,
Silent, still and fathoms deep,
And no sun rise this house upon
Until a hundred years are gone.

"Allah be praised!" the Sultana cried, snatching her child from the cradle.

"The Princess is saved!" the guests exclaimed, embracing each other for joy.

"Oh, queen of fairies!" the Sultan cried as the Twelfth Wise Woman beckoned the others.

"Come, sisters, the hour grows late. We may not tarry beyond midnight. Farewell, mortals, and mortal child. Away, away, away!"

And with each *away* the wise ladies, colour by colour, like a fading rainbow, dissolved into the air.

The Sultan stood gazing, like a man in a dream, at the

nothingness they had left. "Here one moment and gone the next and what have we got to show for it? I meant no harm. As men go, I'm a simple man. All I wanted was a pleasant party, a little family celebration and look at the plight we're in! The Princess Rose is to prick her finger. What did the Wicked Fairy say—a sharp knife, Bouraba?"

"A spindle, High and Mightiness!" Bouraba heaved a sigh.

"Very well, we shall have no spindles. See to it, Vizier! All spindles must be banished from the kingdom. If, within three days, any person is found with a spindle in his possession, I shall cut off his head myself."

The Vizier shuddered and gave his orders and the news ran from mouth to mouth as fire runs from tree to tree.

The old women who herded the sheep, spinning the fleecy thread as they went, clapped their hands to their lips. "What will become of us now?" they cried. "If we do not spin the wool of our sheep what shall we bring to the marketplace to exchange for meat and grain?"

"And what of us?" the weavers asked. "Without wool our looms will be idle."

"And what of us?" the merchants echoed. "Where shall we get our profits?"

"And what of us?" the grandees cried. "We shall be cold without woolen cloaks."

"Is it not strange," said the philosophers, "that so much should be built upon so little; that the organisation of a whole country should depend upon a small piece of carven wood with a metal hook at its end?"

"Alack and alas and farewell spindle!" was the cry throughout the land. The edict was held to be harsh and bitter but everyone bowed before it. No one, however miserable, is anxious to have his head cut off. News came in from all quarters that the spindles had been destroyed.

"Good!" said the Sultan, rubbing his hands. "Since there are now no spindles it stands to reason that my daughter will not find one. And if she does not find a spindle she will not prick her finger. And if she does not prick her finger she will not fall asleep. It is all a question of logic, merely. By this ruse—and I say it without any sense of personal vanity—the Wicked Fairy will be defeated."

How little he knew!

And so the little Princess grew and in such beauty that people would hide their eyes from it for fear of being dazzled.

And as she flourished, so did the country, in spite of the lack of spindles. The old women, having no spinning to do, fell to fashioning flutes of wood or bone. These they took to the market, playing all manner of tunes upon them, and listeners would be so enraptured that each would want a flute for himself. Thus body and soul were kept together.

As for the merchants, they fared as the rich always fare, which is to say well. They sent out stately caravans to bring back woollen cloth from the west, not to mention silk from the east, furs and skins from the far north and linen flax from the south. Thus they grew still richer. And since she was, as it were, the reason for all this well-being, none of them neglected to bring a share of their merchandise to the Princess Rose—a roll of silk for her long trousers, fur slippers for her feet, a linen nightgown, a damask cloak.

For the child, unlike the usual run of princesses—who come and go without making any more stir than a falling pin—was the inner life of the land, the lifeblood of the general vein, the hope of everyone. The people were part of one sentient body of which she was the heart.

Yet for all this she was not puffed-up. The Wise Women had seen to that. Their gifts began to unfold in her as a flower unfolds from its bud. Lovely, healthy, sweet-tempered, joyful, she went upon her childish way, friendly to man and beast. If she had met a tiger, it would have nodded courteously and gone about its business. Her father's camels bowed to her; and this, if you know anything about camels, was a feather in her cap. Cobras would lie in the sun beside her, keeping their hoods neatly folded and their forked tongues tucked away in their mouths.

And ever at her side, as though her body cast a human shadow, was the dark slave, Bouraba. By day she was always in his eye and at night he slept at the door of her chamber. He was not, however, her only playmate. As she grew older she was joined by three other constant companions—a cat that trod always at her heels, a dove that took its seat on her shoulder and a lizard that darted around her feet or skimmed the paths before her.

"This house is becoming a menagerie," the Sultan would say in protest. "I do not care to find a lizard sitting on my soup plate. And I never liked pigeons—except in a pie. As for the cat, its habit of looking at me as though it knew everything and I nothing is distinctly unnerving. Under other circumstances I would simply chop off its head."

He did nothing of the kind, however. If he grumbled it was for the sake of appearances and not to be thought sentimental.

As for the Sultana, nothing that the Princess did could be other than perfect in her eyes. If ever there was a happy woman, it was the Sultana. It never occurred to her to remember that day inevitably turns into night and that what is up must at last come down. If any such thought had crossed her mind she would have contentedly told herself, "My husband is a clever man, as resourceful as he is handsome. If anything should ever happen he will be able to deal with it."

How little she knew!

Happy lives pass swiftly and the Princess Rose grew from child to damsel, almost, it seemed, from one day to the next. And at length the time of maidens was upon her. The lovely bud became lovelier flower and she seemed to waver in the wind, hardly knowing where she was, bending this way and that. Sometimes she would sigh for no reason at all and, if she smiled or became thoughtful, again it would be for no reason. One day it would seem that her father's house, with its great courtyards and soaring domes, was all too small to contain her. And the next she would swing to the opposite pole and wish that the palace would close in and hem her into so small a space that by stretching a hand in any direction she would come upon a wall.

Thus swung between one thing and another, dipping and swaying like a flag in the breeze, she came to her fifteenth birthday.

A feast was made ready in the palace kitchens and as the day brightened, all those who had come to celebrate gathered in the courtyards to prepare for the evening entertainment. Dancers rehearsed their steps and gestures; jugglers practised their legerdemain. Storytellers sought shady corners muttering over to themselves the tales they would tell at dusk. Men from the desert groomed their camels; men from the mountains fingered their bagpipes to keep them in tune for the night.

The whole scene—the palace in the midst of the

embroidered tents and the fields of coloured carpets—was elegant and elaborate. The very air tingled with anticipation. Everyone sensed—it was obvious—that some great event was brewing. "It must be the coming festivity," they whispered vibrantly to each other, "that makes us tremble and hold our breath."

How little they knew!

"Come, my dear," the Sultan said, taking the Sultana by the hand. "Let us go among the people and see that all things are properly disposed. Bouraba, attend upon us!"

So they walked among the bowing throng, over the flowery fields of carpets, and in and out of the tents. Bouraba dawdled at their heels, flinging back glances at the palace like an anxious uneasy dog. Never, since her birth, had he been farther than an arm's length from the Princess and the thought of this tugged at his heart.

"What if she needs me?" he asked himself. And he longed to be standing outside her door awaiting her least command.

But if she had a need of him, the Princess Rose was unaware of it. For now behind that same door she was being robed by her handmaidens. She submitted gravely to their ministrations but her thoughts were far from her fine array and all the preparations. There was a knocking in her mind but where it came from she did not know. Something deep within her said that here she had come to an ending. And as her toilet was completed she rose—with the handmaidens gasping at the sight she made—and left her childhood room.

At once the cat leapt up from its cushion, the dove came swiftly to her shoulder, and the lizard ran round and round her feet.

So accompanied, and as if in a dream, she wandered

through the spacious palace, through council halls and rooms of state, past fountains and shady arbours and courtyards that opened one from another.

For the first time in her life she was alone, accompanied by no human guide, no loving parent nigh, no kind, dark, watchful friend. Four legs ran at her either side and two legs rode on her shoulder as she wandered in her maze of maidenhood. What she sought for she did not know. She only knew that not to find it would leave her incomplete.

At last she came by way of a courtyard she had never seen to the foot of a tower that was equally unknown. And yet it seemed that all her life she had been coming towards it. She began to climb the winding stair, feeling herself drawn up through the tower as a fish is drawn up by the angler's line.

As she came to the edge of the last landing, she heard the sound of music. Somebody close at hand was singing. It sounded like a lullaby, a rising and falling melody with the same phrase repeated again and again. She trembled—was it with fear or joy?—as she tried the handle of a small dark door. Nothing moved. Her fingers felt for the rusted key that grated harshly as she turned it. The door opened with a long slow creak, disclosing a little dark room, empty, it seemed, of all but cobwebs. But the music now was closer at hand, the song repeating without a waver its wheedling lullaby. And gradually, as her eyes became accustomed to the gloom, the Princess descried a curious figure with a cloak drawn over its head. This apparition was seated on a low divan, rocking from side to side. Its hands, making quick and rhythmic movements, glittered and shone in the darkness and the song that came from beneath the cloak seemed to set the cobwebs swaying.

The Princess gazed in astonishment.

"But the door was locked—on the outside! How did you get in?"

The singing ceased. The figure glanced sideways from under its hood as the hands went steadily on with their work, flashing along a woollen thread from which hung a piece of twisting wood.

"There are more ways than one of entering a room," said a soft, alluring voice. "Perhaps," a musical laugh rang out, "I came in through the key-hole."

The Princess took the phrase as a jest.

"I do not think that could be," she said. "And yet—" Her face resumed its dreamy look. "I feel there is something strange here that I do not understand."

"Strange? An old woman sitting all alone with only a mouse for a friend?"

A mouse ran out from the folds of the cloak and the fur of the Princess's cat stiffened.

"I do not think you are old," said the Princess. "Though I cannot see beneath your hood. Your voice is not the voice of age but of someone far away and timeless. I heard your singing and it drew me to you."

"That was my intention," said the voice. "When one has a rendezvous with fate one cannot fail to keep it." The bright hands glittered along the wool till the Princess's eyes were dazzled.

"What is that you are doing?" she asked.

"I am spinning," the silky voice replied. "Spinning a thread upon a spindle."

"And what will you weave from the thread—a gown?"

"A gown—or perhaps a shroud."

"It is an interesting device," said the Princess Rose. "I have never seen a spindle before. I wonder why that is."

24

"Perhaps because your father, child, thinks he is cleverer than he is. Wit is no substitute for wisdom."

The Princess moved forward like one in a trance. "Please may I try it—just for once?"

"Just once, my girl. It only needs once. One twist of the thread. One turn of the hand."

The stranger raised the swinging thread. The Princess bent and took it. And as she tried to set it turning, her hand slipped down along its length and met the spindle's spike.

Out sprang the blood in a red fountain. "Oh, oh," she cried. "I've pricked my finger!"

And at that moment, the cat leapt at the scurrying mouse, the dove went clapping up to the rafters, and the lizard darted across the floor.

"It bleeds," cried the Princess in a daze. "Where are my maids and bodyservants. My mother, father, Bouraba—where? Oh, stranger, help me! What is the matter? I suddenly feel so very sleepy." She yawned behind her bleeding hand and turning about like one in a trance she moved towards the cushions. "I am falling—save me!—into a dream. Goodnight. Goodnight. Goodnight." And with a sigh, she fell in one subsiding movement, stretched herself upon the divan, and was silent.

The cat dropped like a stone to the floor. The dove's head sank upon its breast, the lizard lay still, like a scribble on marble.

"So—so!" A long throaty triumphant laugh came from the folds of the dark cloak as the Thirteenth Wise Woman, moving like waves of violet water, bent over the sleeping girl.

"Did no one warn you, foolish child, to think before you ask? One touch you wanted. One touch was enough

and now the charm's complete. Goodnight, Princess, a long goodnight. A very long goodnight."

And with another exultant laugh, she drew her airy robes about her and swept, like a wisp of purple smoke, straight out through the keyhole.

Now let us see what was happening in the rest of the palace. Curious as it may seem, the fact is that at the moment when the prick of the spindle drew blood from the Princess's finger, the life of the palace came to a complete standstill. The moment she fell asleep, the general eye closed.

The Sultan and the Sultana, returning from their promenade, were entering the Council Chamber when they began to yawn.

"I am afraid," said the Sultana, drowsily, "that I am a little overtired. A rest—huh, huh—will do me good." She turned and was about to depart when she gracefully sank beside the throne, bowed her head on the Sultan's footstool, and there fell fast asleep.

The Sultan was about to remind her to remember her dignity when he, too, collapsed. "Bouraba," he murmured. "Fetch me a cushion. I must sleep now. Wake me in time for the party."

But Bouraba was beyond both cushions and parties. In spite of himself his eyes were closing. In a mighty effort to obey, he fell across his master's knees and at once began to snore.

The same thing happened to everyone else. The Vizier, in the act of writing a death warrant, fell asleep with his cheek on his quill pen. The bowmen, playing at chance in the courtyard, plunged into a deep stupour and their dice hung in the air.

Outside, among the embroidered tents, the storytellers' heads were nodding; acrobats slept in midsomersault; the musicians were all in a deep trance; the camels seemed turned to stone. Even the smoke from the chimneys stood upright and solid in the air. And the fountains froze, not to ice but stillness, with never a drop of water falling.

Hushed and motionless lay the palace. And from the centre where the Princess was, there spread like water round a stone ring upon ring of sleep.

Did I say motionless? I was wrong.

Something moved swiftly through the house. Someone not subject to mortal law swept like a cloud of indigo among the fallen figures.

"Sleep, mortals," said the Twelfth Wise Woman, flashing her golden hands.

> *Sleep, mortals, sleep the time away,*
> *And time shall sleep so that you may*
> *No wrinkle know, nor head of grey.*
> *Then, if you wake well, you will say*
> *A hundred years were but a day,*
> *A hundred years were but a day.*

And as she spoke she became air—she was and she was not. The sun went out, the wind fell, the flags hung motionless on the flagpoles. Darkness fell on the sleeping palace and round it rose, in the wink of an eye, an enclosing hedge of thorn. No one could have guessed that behind those battlements of briar there lay a living rose.

That is how it all happened. And for a time it was a matter for wonder. The firesides of every hut and mansion were busy with the news. What could it mean? Why had it happened? And how would it all work out?

And then, of course, it was forgotten—except for an old wife here and there who would tell her grandchildren a strange story of a princess sleeping behind the thorns. And the grandchildren told it to their children till at last it became a fairy tale, something forever true but far. Men came to think of the Princess, not as a person anymore, but as a secret within themselves—a thing they would dearly wish to discover if they could but make the effort.

There was one family, however, that preserved the story in all its detail. Poor people they were, without book learning and able, perhaps for that very reason, to remember things exactly. These were the woodcutters who lived beside the hedge.

It had so happened that in the days when the Princess was a child, the woodcutter's son had caught a moment's glimpse of her as she played under a cypress tree. And the effect she made upon him was such that he took a seed of the cypress tree and planted it in his father's garden to remind him of her for evermore. Later, when he himself became a father, he told his son of how he had seen the Princess Rose and all that ultimately befell. This son, in turn, told *his* son and thus it was that the woodcutters became, so to speak, the guardians of the story and also of the great dark hedge. Father to son, they told the tale and hung their jerkins on the spines of the wall and warned any would-be hero of the dangers of trying to pass within it.

For, of course, in every generation, some of the children who had heard the story grew up into brave young men who were ready to put their courage to the test, stake their lives for the unknown maiden, and make an assault on the hedge.

But all to no avail. No sword prevailed against the thorn. The bristling wall turned back all weapons and the briars stretched out their barbed hands and clasped the heroes to them. There they would struggle, crying aloud for help and pity, dying at last in the pronged arms, their bodies clipped to the boughs, like fruit.

And the passers-by, seeing the corpses on the hedge, would note the costly price of valour and congratulate themselves that they had not been similarly foolhardy. "It is better," they told themselves, "to sleep in bed with a sure wife, however homely, than to lose one's life for a mythical mistress, however fine and fair." And for all one knows, they were right.

What is time? We live in it but never see it. From here to there it carries us but we neither taste, hear, smell, nor touch it. How, then, can we describe its passage? By watching something grow, perhaps, or watching something fade.

Think of the woodcutter's cypress seed. After a season in the earth it sends up a small white thread. Then the sun gets to work on it and changes the white to green. "Look, it has sprouted!" cries the woodcutter's son. And, since cypress trees are long in growing, he grows old watching the sprout become a sapling. And watching the sapling become a tree his son, too, grows old. Generation after generation, the woodcutters watch the tree thicken and stretch its branches upwards. Till at last it attains its full height and shows us the shape of time.

Yearly the tree's shadow lengthened and there came a day when it reached the hedge. And at the same moment the charm that had been set in motion by the Wicked Fairy completed its full circle.

The day was heavy and slow to move. A mottle of clouds hung over the sun. Men in their pointed turned-up slippers dragged one foot after another. "What can be the matter?" they asked each other. "We seem to be waiting for something." And they longed for the day to come to an end so that what was to be might disclose itself.

At length it was over. The water clocks, filling one bowl from another, drop by drop wore the hours away— noon to sunset, sunset to dark.

The woodcutter, grandson many times removed of the one who had planted the cypress seed, settled himself at the edge of the thorn hedge, with his axe across his knees. Here he would wait, as his ancestors had done before him, to guard and watch and warn.

Meanwhile, by road and desert, field and mountain, a young prince from a distant land was marching to that selfsame spot. And if before him through the night there flowed a cloudy indigo shape with head and foot of flashing gold, he had no notion of it. He strode on all unseeing— looking perhaps within himself, as though he were his own compass and was drawn by his own fate.

The woodcutter stirred at the sound of footsteps.

"Who goes there?" he demanded sharply.

"I am a prince from a far country. I have come to seek the Sleeping Princess."

"Then I beg you, Prince, heed my warning. Turn your steps from this fearful place, lest you suffer the fate of all those who were once the sons of kings."

The woodcutter waved his axe at the hedge where the white bones hung in the branches. Chalky hands, still wearing jewels, gripped at the fronds of briar. Crowned skulls bent, grinning, from the thorns. Tatters of turban, cloak, and slipper, tarnished from their original brightness, waved in the midnight breeze.

"A king of China hangs there," said the woodcutter,

"and a prince from the Western Sea; potentates from India; khans from the hills and deserts. Begone while there is time, young lord, lest you, too, leave your bones on the thorn."

"Everyone must die," said the Prince. "I would rather leave my bones here than in any other place."

The woodcutter sighed. "Many a youth has spoken so and yet gone to his death. Besides, Prince, you are all unarmed. No knife, no sword, no spear, no sickle. How will you cut a path through the hedge?"

"I am indeed, all unarmed. But all my life, without ceasing, I have bent my thought to this quest."

"Well, it shall not be said that I failed to warn you. Do as you will and must."

The dead twigs crackled under his feet as the Prince strode towards the hedge.

The woodcutter made one last effort. "Prince, beware!" he said, anxiously—and then stood rooted to the earth, mouth open, hand in air.

For as the Prince drew near the hedge the thorny tendrils broke apart like a skein that is unravelled. The spiky branches loosed their hold, the great trunks leaned away from each other, making an open pathway. And as the Prince stepped through the gap every bough and frond and twig burst into buds and flowers.

A great shine lit the woodcutter's eyes as he realised what had happened.

"He is himself his own weapon. The time must be ripe," he said. And he ran as fast as his legs would go to tell the news to his wife.

"The hundred years are gone!" he shouted, swinging his axe round his head.

"Are gone, are gone!" ticked the water clocks. And everywhere in towns and villages, in desert tents and in mountain caves, men stirred a little in their sleep, knowing that something new had happened.

Meanwhile, the Prince marched through the forest and as he went the boughs broke out in fountains of bloom and all that had been knotted and tied was loosened and set free. Every barbed and spreading briar, locked to another in a long embrace, gave up its thorny partner and parted to let him pass. As the last branch fell away he stepped out of the hedge's shadow and beheld the sleeping palace.

Veils of dust hung upon the briars, the dust of years littered the thorn forest, but the palace lay there all untouched by earth mould or the mould of time.

The first dawn for a hundred years was breaking as the Prince picked his way among the sleepers. It shone on coloured tents and carpets, on plump cheeks and glossy hair, all fresh and all unfaded.

Ducking his head under the jugglers' hoops which were still hanging in the air, the Prince skirted the acrobats, asleep with their legs over their heads; hurried past nodding storytellers and leapt over the snoring camels. In the portico he passed the guards, all sprawling against the pillars. And at last he came to the Council Chamber.

Before the throne the Prince paused, folded his hands together and bowed. For though the Sultan, lolling sideways among his cushions was all unaware of his visitor, nevertheless he was a king. And kings, as the Prince well knew, are entitled to obeisance.

But such courtesies were, for the Prince, merely a matter of form. As he bowed, his eyes swept round the hall, searching its every corner. There lay Bouraba on the

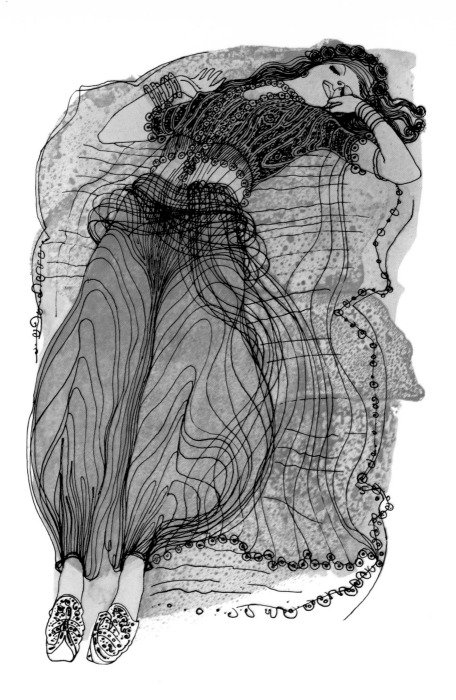

Sultan's knees; the Sultana, fine as a fine painting, asleep with her cheek upon the footstool and her maidens all about her. But the Prince's gaze did not linger. Something nearer than his inmost pulse told him that she whom he had so long sought was not within the chamber. He pushed aside an embroidered curtain and continued on his way.

For just as the Princess Rose, a hundred years ago, had been drawn by the magnet of her fate, so she herself became the magnet that drew the Prince to his. Steadfast as the compass needle that ever points to the north he moved through chamber and corridor, noting everything he passed but lingering not a moment.

As he passed through it, the palace, as though it were a single body, seemed to rise and fall with the sleeping breaths. And the courtyards rang with his living footsteps as he passed the moveless fountains.

At last, drawn by an unseen thread, he came to the foot of the tower. He glanced upwards and without a moment's hesitation set his foot on the winding stair. The blue gleam that heralds sunrise shone through the narrow windows and he moved alternately through light and shadow as he took the stairs three at a stretch and came to the upper landing.

And there, for the first time, he paused, as though to gather in himself an even, easy flow of breath and all his lifelong purpose. Then he gently opened the creaking door and entered the little room.

There lay the Princess, hand to cheek, and at this sight the heart of the Prince lost one beat in its fearful joy. He knew himself to be at the centre of the world and that, in him, all men stood there, gazing at their hearts' desire—or perhaps their inmost selves. He trembled—aghast at his own daring. A lesser man would perhaps have fled but not for nothing had he spent his life preparing for this moment. The coward tremour passed away and his courage came flowing back. Silently, he vowed to serve the accomplishment as he had served the quest. Then he took a stride towards the divan and bent to kiss the Princess.

She drew a deep shuddering breath, opened her eyes, and smiled.

"I have been dreaming about you," she said, simply. For indeed, what else had been her preoccupation all these sleeping years? "And now," she yawned behind her hand, "now my dream has come true."

Silently he kissed her again and together they plumbed all height, all depth, and rose up strongly to the surface, back to the shores of time.

At the same moment the sun rose and spread like a fan across the house it had not looked on for a hundred years. An awakening sigh, rising as from a single throat, stirred throughout the palace. Fountains trembled and loosed their waters; pennons flapped on the flagpoles. Down in the courtyards the acrobats suddenly leapt to their feet, the jugglers' hoops fell into their hands. Everyone was refreshed and lively as people are who have slept well.

And destiny resumed its course. The Vizier woke and signed his paper. The cook at long last struck the kitchen boy, and the kitchen maid, without even a yawn, plucked out another feather. The die in the portico fell from the air and the bowmen woke and bent above it and found it had turned up a six.

In the Council Chamber the Sultan grunted, flexing his arms as men do when they first wake in the morning. Then he opened his eyes and looked about him.

The first thing he saw was the Sultana, who, gathering her filmy veil about her, was rising from the floor.

"My dear," he said, with a hint of sternness—for he was a great stickler for the proprieties. "If you had to fall asleep in the daytime, would it not have been more appropriate to do so in your retiring chamber and not, like any handmaiden, stretched out upon the carpet?"

"It would, indeed," she agreed gently, for she knew better than to make a molehill out of what her husband considered a mountain. "But something came over me like a cloud and I seemed to fade away. You yawn and sigh yourself, my lord. Is it not possible that you, too, may have slept a little?"

"Oh, a second, perhaps. Just forty winks. One so burdened with cares of state may nod from time to time." The Sultan's eyes were closing again.

"And Bouraba," said the Sultana, slyly. "Does he have cares of state as well?"

The Sultan opened his eyes and stared. The expression on his face was awesome.

"Bou-ra-ba!" he spluttered furiously. "How dare you fall asleep in my presence? And what is more, upon my knee—the knee of one whose cousin's cousin is descended from the Prophet! Down, dog, and let me strike off your head."

"Oh, dear, oh dear, what is amiss?" The handmaidens, waking from their sleep, twittered like frightened birds.

"Allah, defend me!" cried Bouraba, waking from sleep with a loud groan, and prostrating himself before the throne.

The Sultan snatched the sword from his thigh and was just about to swing it downwards when the Sultana put out her hand.

The Sultan, she knew, was hasty-tempered. She also

had good reason to know that his bark was worse than his bite. If he beheaded his slave today, he would rue the act tomorrow.

"Would it not be better," she suggested, "to put it off till later? Let him assist at the birthday feast and, if you are still of the same mind, you can kill him when it is over."

"Birthday? What birthday?" the Sultan demanded, putting a hand to his brow. "Oh, now, I remember. My daughter is fifteen today and we are celebrating. All right, I'll wait until tomorrow. I shall not be so busy then. Stand up, Bouraba! Cease this foolish groaning. Go to the Princess Rose's apartments, remind her that the hour grows late and bid her join us here."

Bouraba staggered to his feet, took a step towards the door, and fell to his knees again.

"Get up!" said the Sultan, testily. "How dare you kneel when I bid you rise. Stop grovelling, Bouraba, do, and hurry to fetch my daughter."

"I am here!" said a familiar voice, as everyone turned to the doorway.

A cry of wonder broke from them all, from ladies-in-waiting, courtiers, guards as they made their deep salaams. For it seemed, if such a thing could be, that the Princess was lovelier than ever. She stood and shone in her own light and dazzled everyone.

"Oh!" the Sultana murmured raptly, putting her hand before her eyes.

But the Sultan, though he, too, sensed his child's new beauty, was determined not to show it.

"Ah, there you are," he said, airily. "And, really, about time, too. May I remind you that it is not becoming in a princess to be late for any event, particularly a birthday

39

party. Do not let it occur—" he was about to say "again" when his eye fell upon the handsome figure that was standing behind his daughter.

"But who is this?" he demanded, sternly. "What stranger dares to enter my house without addressing himself to me? Come forth, young man, and declare yourself!"

The Prince obeyed, smiling, and so handsome was he, so bright with inward triumph, that it was all the handmaidens could do not to swoon away at the sight of him.

"Do not be angry, Father dear," the Princess pleaded, softly. "He is the son of the King of the Silver Mountain. And he came through the enchanted forest to wake us all from sleep."

"The Silver Mountain!" the Sultan gasped, for he knew that the King of the Silver Mountain was the richest king in the world. "You are indeed a welcome guest. But as for waking us all from sleep—with all due respect, Prince—though I dare say you meant it kindly—we here are like other human beings. We sleep or wake as the case may be, exactly when we wish."

"Not so, dear Father," the Princess murmured, kneeling at the Sultan's side. And then she told the whole story while he, the Sultana and their attendants listened—not, of course, open-mouthed for that would hardly have been compatible with etiquette—but with extreme amazement.

"This is preposterous!" cried the Sultan. "There must be some mistake. I ordered all spindles out of the kingdom. Who would disobey me? This person hidden in a cloak, spinning and singing—ridiculous! And as for sleeping a hundred years, you must have dreamed it, child! You have been taking a little nap, just like your mother and myself and that foolish slave, Bouraba."

The Sultana gazed thoughtfully at her daughter as she put out her hand to her husband.

"A woman wrapped in a violet robe whose hand flashed bright as silver. Who wears such garments, in our acquaintance? Who bears such a hand?"

"The Thirteenth Wise Woman!" The Sultan stared. "But no, it can't be. I merely nodded. And what is this talk of enchanted forests? You will have seen for yourself, Prince, that our land is wild and stony. Few trees take root upon the rock. There are no forests here."

The Prince gestured towards the windows. "If Your Highness would be so gracious—" he said, with a generous sweep of his hand.

The Sultan turned, his eye ready for craggy landscapes and a few sparse cypress trees. But instead of that familiar scene, a strange sight met his eyes.

"A forest of thorns! I can't believe it. No, no, I won't be made a fool of. I shall be a laughing-stock to my neighbours if I listen to taradiddles."

His glance shifted uneasily from the Prince to the forest and back again. He was troubled—and who can blame him? It is not everyone who can be ready for anything at any moment.

"Besides," he continued, trying to bring the whole matter within the realm of reason. "If we had slept for a hundred years, we should now appear quite different. My wife would be a withered crone, my daughter almost as old and ugly. And I, though I am well-preserved, would be at least a greybeard. And look at us!" He lovingly stroked his fine black beard. "No one can deny that we are in the prime of life. If we slept, then time slept, Prince, and that could never happen."

"And time shall sleep," the Sultana murmured.

Time shall sleep so that you may
No wrinkle know, nor head of gray.

She nodded wisely to herself, for slowly things were coming back to her.

"What's that? Absurd! A foolish rhyme! And yet—yes, there was another line:

Then, if you wake well, you will say
A hundred years were but a day.

That's it! It all comes back to me. The Twelfth Wise Woman waved her hand and after that—nothing. We must have fallen asleep at once. And now, after a hundred years, we indeed have woken well. What an extraordinary event! Everything has come true!" You would never have guessed from the Sultan's manner that not five minutes ago he had spoken of taradiddles.

"Everything," echoed the Princess softly, exchanging with the Prince a look that was like a silent vow.

"Well, Prince," said the Sultan, who now felt himself to be fully in command of the situation. "Let us get down to more serious matters. If my eyes do not deceive me, sir, you wish to marry my daughter."

"Nothing on earth could prevent my doing so." The Prince made a deep salaam.

"Then she is yours!" declared the Sultan. And he rubbed his hands gleefully at the thought of all the gold and silver that would pour into his coffers. "Take her to your own land and when, in due course, she bears a son, he shall reign here in my stead. Everything works for the best, you see. A prick of the finger was a small price to pay for such an outcome. Really, I need not have worried."

But as to whether he was right about this, I must leave you to judge. It is difficult at any time to know what is small and what is great.

"And remind me, Bouraba," the Sultan continued. "To send an acknowledgment to the Twelfth Wise Woman. For it is to that good lady—not to mention my own sagacity—that we owe our present fortune."

It did not occur to him to remember that had he been truly sagacious he would also have sent an acknowledgment to the Thirteenth Wise Woman. A wise man would have recognised that it was she who, by putting the situation in danger, called forth the rescuing power. Light is light because of the dark and the Sultan should have known it.

He was, however, a busy man with little time for thinking; and soon he was giving orders that the meats baked for the Princess's birthday should furnish forth her wedding feast.

The marriage was celebrated at once—for what was there to wait for?—and those who had gathered to entertain the maiden now paraded their talents before the bride.

And when the last carpet was rolled up, the last song sung, the Princess Rose turned away. She bowed to her parents and received their blessing. Then she took her husband's hand.

And he who had kissed her from sleep to waking, now led her from her childhood world towards the great hedge of thorns and the path he had taken through it.

In silence the parents watched them go till the bowing branches took them in and hid them from all eyes.

"Well, that's that," said the Sultan, grandly. "I've had a long pleasant sleep, I have found my daughter a perfect husband and a rich ally for myself. All is well that ends well, as I have always said."

The Sultana smiled. She could not recollect that he had ever made such a statement. Nor did she feel it a propitious moment to remind him that it was not *he* who had found the Prince. So she said nothing.

At the same time she could not help wondering about all that had happened. And from that day forward, since she now had time and leisure for it, she pondered and dreamed and questioned. And the more she thought about it, the more it seemed that her daughter had stepped, as it were, into another dimension—into, in fact, a fairy tale. And if this were so, she told herself, she would have to look for the meaning. For she knew very well that fairy tales are not as simple as they appear; that the more innocent and candid they seem, the wilier one has to be in one's efforts to find out what they are up to.

So pondering, she would sit under the cypress tree, secretly telling herself the story and hoping that the story at last would tell its secret to her. Who was the maiden, who the Prince, and what the thorny hedge? And then she would tire of all such questions and just sit thinking of nothing, till the Sultan called her back to the world or Bouraba came with the peacock fan, holding it high above her head for fear she should take a sunstroke . . . .

As for the newly wedded pair, they moved along the flower-decked path with the thorn boughs curtseying before them. And ever about them as in a dance, light and shadow flickered and gleamed as the sun dappled the forest. Were there, I wonder, among the sunshafts, bright flashes of another kind—of gold head and silver foot and a dazzle of rainbow shapes? Indeed, I think it very likely.

There is no good love without good luck and what more fitting than that the Thirteen Wise Women who had played so potent a part in the story should accompany their mortal nurselings on the first stage of their journey, to bring the fairy tale to a close and fortune to the lovers?

What, *all* of them? do I hear you ask? And I reply, of course! Violet is as necessary to the rainbow as any of the other colours. It is either the beginning or the end, depending how you look at it. At any rate it completes the spectrum.

Thus accompanied, the Prince led the Princess to the edge of the forest. And as they passed through the last green arch the hedge trembled and disappeared. One moment it was standing there and the next moment— nothing. No thorn, no briar, no twig, no seed. Nor was there any further flash of golden head or foot. When a pearl is in safekeeping there is no more need of locks and bars. When the Wise Women have performed one duty they hasten away to another.

The way lay clear ahead now and the lovers walked it hand in hand, bringing what secrets they had learned down to the world of men. And so they came to the villages, to the towns and marketplaces, for it is only in the world of men that it is possible to live happily ever after. There lies the test of every hero and the outcome of his quest. All stories continue and end there and so does this of the Sleeping Beauty.

And the one who last told it is still living, still feels the sunlight and heeds the rain, glory be to Allah!

Afterword

Are there thirteen Wise Women at every christening? I think it very likely. I think, too, that whatever gifts they give are over and above those that life offers. If it is beauty it is of some supplementary kind that is not dependent on fine eyes and a perfect nose, though it may include these features. If it is wealth, it comes from some inner abundance that has no relation to pearls and rubies, though the lucky ones may get these, too.

I shall never know which good lady it was who, at my own christening, gave me the everlasting gift, spotless amid all spotted joys, of love for the fairy tale. It began in me quite early, before there was any separation between myself and the world. Eve's apple had not yet been eaten; every bird had an emperor to sing to and any passing ant or beetle might be a prince in disguise.

This undifferentiated world is common to all children.

They may never have heard of the fairy tales but still be on easy terms with myth. Saint George and King Arthur, under other names, defend the alleyways and crossroads, and Beowulf's Grendel, variously disguised, breathes fire in the vacant lots. Skipping games, street songs, lullabies, all carry the stories in them. But far above these, as a source of myth, are the half-heard scraps of gossip, from parent to parent, neighbour to neighbour as they whisper across a fence. A hint, a carefully garbled disclosure, a silencing finger at the lip, and the tales, like rain clouds, gather. It could almost be said that a listening child has no need to read the tales. A keen ear and the power to dissemble—he must not *seem* to be listening—are all that is required. By putting two and two together—fragments of talk and his own logic—he will fashion the themes for himself.

For me, the nods and becks of my mother's friends, walking under parasols or presiding over tinkling tea-tables, were preparatory exercises to my study of the myths. The scandals, the tight corners, the flights into the face of fate! When eventually I read of Zeus visiting Danaë in a shower of gold, Perseus encountering the Gorgon, or the hair-breadth escapes of the Argonauts, such adventures caused me no surprise. I had heard their modern parallels over tea and caraway cake.

As for the Three Fates, I recognised them immediately as my great-aunts, huge cloudy presences—with power, it seemed, to loose and to bind—perched watchfully, like crows on a fence, at the edge of our family circle. One of them, it was said—or rather, it was whispered, the rumour being so hideous—one of them lived on her capital. What was capital, I wondered, wild with conjecture, full of concern. And the dreadful answer came bubbling up—it was *herself*, her substance! Each day she disappeared to her room, it was not to rest, like anyone else, but secretly to live on her person, to gnaw, perhaps, a toe or a finger or to wolf down some inner organ. The fact that there was no visible sign of this activity did not fool me for a moment. A strange and dreadful deed was here and not to be denied. Aunt Jane, stealthily nibbling at her liver, was at once her own Prometheus and her own eagle. The myth did not need to be told me. It rose and spoke itself.

I might have saved myself anxiety by taking the question to my parents who would have expounded the role of capital in the world of things-as-they-are. But the grown-up view of things-as-they-are, limited as it is in dimension, lit by a wholly rational sun and capable of explanation, is different from that of a child. For a child this world is infinite, the sun shines up from the abyss as well as down from the sky, the time is always now and endless and the only way to explain a thing is to say that it cannot be explained.

I am glad, therefore, to have kept my terror whole and thus retained a strong link with the child's things-as-they-are, where all things relate to one another and all are congruous. Hercules, the Frog Prince, and Joseph in his coloured coat march with the child to Babylon by candle-light and back.

The boy who assured me that the Virgin Mary was the mother of Finn, the Irish hero—reasoning, perhaps, that all princely paladins must be born from a single stock—was in this world well within his rights. So, too, was the one who hoped—and not at all hopelessly—that since Castor and Pollux were turned at death into neighbour stars, the same courtesy might well be shown to himself and his nearest and dearest. And both would have had a brotherly feeling for the little girl who, assured at bedtime that she need not feel lonely—the One Above being everywhere—begged her mother earnestly to ask God to leave the room. "He makes me nervous," she protested. "I would rather have Rumpelstiltzkin." This form of thinking, which perhaps should properly be called linking, is the essence of fairy tale. All things may be included in it.

Perhaps we are born knowing the tales for our grandmothers and all their ancestral kin continually run about in our blood repeating them endlessly, and the shock they give us when we first hear them is not of surprise but of recognition. Things long unknowingly known have suddenly been remembered. Later, like streams, they run underground. For a while they disappear and we lose them. We are busy, instead, with our personal myth in which the real is turned to dream and the dream becomes the real. Sifting all this is a long process. It may perhaps take half a lifetime and the few who come round to the tales again are those who are in luck.

But love of the fairy tales, you may argue, need not require the lover to refashion them. Do they need retelling, you may ask. Does it not smack of arrogance for any writer to imagine he can put a gloss on a familiar theme? If I answer yes to both these questions I put myself in jeopardy. And yet, why should I fear? To be in jeopardy is a proper fairy-tale situation. Danger is at the heart of the matter, for without danger how shall we foster the rescuing power?

Besides, is it not true that the fairy tale has always been in a continuous process of transformation? How else can we account for the widely differing versions that turn up in different countries? One cannot say of any of the Sleeping Beauties in this book that here is the sole and absolute source, if, indeed, such a thing exists.

The idea of the sleeper, of somebody hidden from mortal eye, waiting until the time shall ripen has always been dear to the folkly mind—Snow White asleep in her glass coffin, Brynhild behind her wall of fire, Charlemagne in the heart of France, King Arthur in the Isle of Avalon, Frederick Barbarossa under his mountain in Thuringia. Muchukunda, the Hindu King, slept through eons till he was awakened by the Lord Krishna; Oisin of Ireland dreamed in Tir n'an Og for over three hundred years. Psyche in her magic sleep is a type of Sleeping Beauty, Sumerian Ishtar in the underworld may be said to be another. Holga the Dane is sleeping and waiting, and so, they say, is Sir Francis Drake. Quetzalcoatl of Mexico and Virochocha of Peru are both sleepers. Morgan le Fay of France and England and Dame Holle of Germany are sleeping in raths and cairns.

The theme of the sleeper is as old as the memory of man. Where it first arose we do not know. One can never find where myth and fairy tale begin any more than one can find wild wheat growing. They are not invented, that is certain. They germinate from seeds sown by an unknown hand. "The Authors," as the poet William Blake has said, "are in Eternity," and we must be content to leave them there. The story is, after all, what matters.

It is true, of course, that all of the five versions gathered here can be dated; that is, we know when they were first published. The Italian Gianbattista Basile's *Pentamerone* which gives us *"Sole, Luna, e Talia"* belongs to the early part of the seventeenth century; Charles Perrault's *"La Belle au Bois Dormant,"* the French version, to the latter part. Grimm's *"Dornroschen"* first found its way into print in Germany in the early nineteenth century, Bradley-Birt's "The Petrified Mansion," from Bengal, and Jeremiah Curtin's "The Queen of Tubber Tintye," from Ireland, in the nineteenth century's closing years. But every one of these historically authenticated persons was a collector, not a creator. They retold, in their own words, stories that were told to them. But the theme itself, the theme of the Sleeper, has no relation to historical fact; it comes from afar, from the world's storehouse of fairy tale which is somewhere beyond the calendar.

This being so, I have grouped the stories of The Sleeping Beauty, not in order of precedence—there is no way of knowing which came first—but in relation to each other. For instance, "The Petrified Mansion" and "The Queen of Tubber Tintye" have in common the fact that in both versions animals as well as humans fall under the spell of sleep. There is a further link between these two in that in neither story is there any foretelling of the heroine's fate, nor any mention of the spinning motif. In turn, "The Queen of Tubber Tintye" has an element in common with *"Sole, Luna, e Talia,"* for in both tales the Prince "steals the fruit of love" while the Beauty lies asleep. Perrault rectifies this by providing a chapel and a priest so that hero and heroine may be lawfully married. Even so, *"Sole, Luna, e Talia"* and *"La Belle au Bois Dormant"* have several similar characteristics. In each the fate of the Beauty is foretold, by astrologers in Basile, by the Fairies in Perrault; in each, two children are begotten; in each the Prince is provided with an ogress relative who orders the children to be slain and served up in a stew—in Basile a wife, in Perrault a mother.

This last motif does not appear in *"Dornroschen"*—indeed, as the Brothers Grimm so clearly saw, it is not necessary to the fundamental theme and probably does not belong to it. But in Grimm the spindle is retained from *"La Belle au Bois Dormant"*; so also are Perrault's Fairies, though these are transmogrified in the German version into Thirteen Wise Women.

In this latest, and best known, telling of the story it is possible to see how over the centuries it has been refined and purged of dross. It is as though the tale itself, through its own energy and need, had winnowed away everything but the true whole grain. By the time it was told to the Brothers Grimm, its outer stuff, worked on by time and the folkly mind, had become transparent and complete, nothing too much, nothing too little. Bradly-Birt's stark narrative has been elaborated; Jeremiah Curtin's over-wordiness has been curbed; Basile's gross justification for his gross events—that fortune brings luck to those that sleep—is seen for the graceless thing it is and dropped accordingly; Perrault's sophistries fall away and the story emerges clear, all essence.

It is this version, this clarification of the tale on which I have built what one may call the Sultana's interpretation. It was written not at all to improve the story—how could one improve on the Brothers Grimm?—but to ventilate my own thoughts about it. To begin with, I was at pains to give it a faraway setting—a vaguely Middle-Eastern world—to lift it out of its well-worn rut. I needed to separate it from its attic clutter—the spinning wheel, the pointed witch cap and all the pantomime buffoonery—in order to see its meaning clear. The story in its present guise may be thought of as a series of reflections on the theme of the

Sleeping Beauty, particularly as it appears in *"Dorn-roschen"* (Rose in the Thorns or Briar Rose).

The opening theme is a familiar one. The King and the Queen, like our Sultan and Sultana, are longing for a child. This situation is so often and so insistently restated in the fairy tales that we cannot but take notice of it. What is it telling us? That in fairy tale, compared with the rest of the teeming world, the characters are less fecund? Surely not. The child is withheld in order to show the need for what the child stands for—the new order, the renewed conditions, the throwing forward of events, the revivifying of life. Once this need is made clear the longing is allowed to bear its proper fruit. In Perrault, after "prayers, pilgrimages, vows to saints," the Queen at last conceives. But note what happens in Grimm. A frog brings her the reassurance. Within a year, she will bear a child. A messenger rises from the dark waters where all things have their beginnings. In effect, her own unconsciousness speaks.

So, in due time, the child is born, the new events begin to gather, and the story is on its way. The christening, the first rite of passage in any life, has now to be performed. And since the good graces of the fairy world are essential to any mortal undertaking, the Wise Women are sent for. Here now is the first hint of danger, the hand-sized cloud in the sky. For while there are thirteen Wise Women in the kingdom, the King has only twelve gold places. What a foolish short-sighted man to put himself in such a position!

But we must not forget that there has to be a story. A fairy tale like any other, has its own organic life that may not be shortened or cut down before its allotted span. Where would the story be if the King had been wiser and had had a little forethought? Or if, going back a little farther, the child had not been born? To find the meaning we need the story and once we have accepted the story we cannot escape the story's fate.

Well, what does the King do? In Perrault he provides seven gold cases for seven Fairies, believing that the eighth Fairy was under a spell or dead or somehow harmless. (It is typical of Perrault that for all his sophistry he was unaware that creatures of the fairy world are known to be immortal.) Grimm merely notes, without attempting to solve the problem, that as there were only twelve gold plates one of the Thirteen Wise Women would have to stay at home. In our version, the Sultan, indeed, senses the danger but washes his hands of responsibility and leaves the matter to chance. He could, perhaps, have borrowed a plate or sent for a goldsmith and had one made. But the story had to have its way and the Thirteenth Wise Woman her opportunity.

The appearance of this lady at the christening is the great moment of the tale, the hook from which everything hangs. Properly to understand why this is so we must turn to Wise Women in general and their role in the world of men. To begin with they are not mortal women. They are sisters, rather, of the Sirens, kin to the Fates and the World Mothers. As such, as creatures of another dimension, myth and legend have been at pains to embody them in other than human shape—the winged female figures of Homer, the bird-headed women of the Irish tales, the wild women of ancient Russia with square heads and hairy bodies and the wisplike Jinn of the Middle East who were not allowed grosser forms than those of fire and smoke. It was to do away with their pantomime image and give them their proper weight and authority that our version provided the

Wise Women with their hairless heads of gold and silver and made their golden and silver feet hover a little above the earth as the gods do on the Greek vases. And in dressing them in the colours of the spectrum, the aim was to suggest that the Thirteen are parts of the single whole and the opposites complementary.

For it should be remembered that no Wise Woman or Fairy is in herself either good or bad; she takes on one aspect or the other according to the laws of the story and the necessity of events. The powers of these ladies are equivocal. They change with changing circumstances; they are as swift to take umbrage as they are to bestow a boon; they curse and bless with equal gusto. Each Wise Woman is, in fact, an aspect of the Hindu goddess, Kali, who carries in her multiple hands the powers of good and evil.

It is clear, therefore, that the Thirteenth Wise Woman becomes the Wicked Fairy solely for the purposes of one particular story. It was by chance that she received no invitation; it might just as well have been one of her sisters. So, thrust by circumstance into her role, she acts according to law.

Up she rises, ostensibly to avenge an insult but in reality to thrust the story forward and keep the drama moving. She becomes the necessary antagonist, placed there to show that whatever is "other," opposite and fearful, is as indispensable an instrument of creation as any force for good. The pulling of the Devas and Asuras in opposite directions churn the ocean of life in the Hindu myth and the interaction of the good and the bad Fairies produces the fairy tale. The Thirteenth Wise Woman stands as a guardian of the threshold, the paradoxical adversary without whose presence no threshold may be passed.

This is the role played in so many stories by the Wicked Stepmother. The true mother, by her very nature, is bound to preserve, protect and comfort; this is why she is so often disposed of before the story begins. It is the stepmother, her cold heart unwittingly cooperating with the hero's need, who thrusts the child from the warm hearth, out from the sheltering walls of home to find his own true way.

Powers such as these, at once demonic and divine, are not to be taken lightly. They give a name to evil, free it, and bring it into the light. For evil will out, they sharply warn us, no matter how deeply buried. Down in its dungeon it plots and plans, waiting, like an unloved child, the day of its revenge. What it needs, like the unloved child, is to be recognised, not disclaimed; given its place and proper birthright and allowed to contact and cooperate with its sister beneficent forces. Only the integration of good and evil and the stern acceptance of opposites will change the situation and bring about the condition that is known as Happy Ever After.

Without the Wicked Fairy there would have been no story. She, not the heroine, is the goddess in the machine. Her hand is discernible in every event that leads up to the denouement; the departure of the protecting parents from the palace on the day of the birthday, the inner promptings that lead the princess to climb the fateful tower, and who can deny—though it is never explicitly stated in any of the three versions dealing with the spinning motif—that the Thirteenth Wise Woman and none other is the old woman with the spindle? Fairy tales have a logic of their own and that the Wicked Fairy should take upon herself this role is a logical assumption. So mighty a character would inevitably play her part out to the very end.

For me she has always been unique among the shadow figures of the stories. As a child I had no pity for the jealous queen in "Snow White" or the shifty old witch in "Rapunzel." I could cheerfully consign all the cruel stepmothers to their cruel fates. But the ill luck of the Wicked Fairy roused all my child's compassion. She was, in a sense, a victim. For her alone there was no gold plate—all she could do was accept the fact. But there was a certain nobility in her acceptance. Without complaining, well aware of the fact that things must go wrong that they may come right, she undertook the task that made her the most despised figure in all fairy tale, the one least worthy of forgiveness. All I could do, in the face of the tragedy, was to comfort myself with the thought that in another story, at another time, the Thirteenth Wise Woman would be avenged. Her luck would at last come round again: chance would give her a golden plate, chance would give her the possibility of playing the part of the Good Fairy.

But it is not only the nobility of the Wicked Fairy that makes "The Sleeping Beauty" unique among fairy tales. The story also contains the one hero who appears to have no hero's task to perform. The Prince has to slay no dragon in order to win the hand of the Princess. There is no dwarf or talking animal to befriend, no glass mountain to be climbed. All he has to do is to come at the right time. The Grimm version alone mentions the fact that the hedge was hung with the corpses of those who had tried to break through before the hundred years were up, thus pointing an admonitory finger at the truth that to choose the moment when the time is ripe is essentially a hero deed. So, all unarmed, the Prince arrives. The time, the place, and the man coincide. He walks through the bowing, flowering hedge as easily as Arthur, the Once and Future King, pulls the royal sword from the stone. The Prince is the sole hero of fairy tale for whom it is a question not of doing but of being. In a word, he is himself his own task. Only such a one, Perrault and Grimm both wordlessly tell us, can give the kiss that will break the spell.

But if the Prince is a mysterious figure, how much more so is she who is the crux of the story, the maiden of surpassing beauty asleep behind her wall of thorns, she whom men from the beginning of time have pondered on and treasured. I say the beginning of time with intent, for when a woman is the chief character in a story it is a sign of the theme's antiquity. It takes us back to those cloudy eras when the world was ruled not, as it was in later years, by a god but by the Great Goddess. Here, as with the Prince, is a heroine who has ostensibly nothing to do, nothing to suffer. She is endowed with every blessing by grace and happy fortune, no slights or indignities are put upon her as is the case with her sister heroines, Snow White, Cinderella, Little Two-Eyes, or the Goose Girl. She simply has to follow her fate, prick her finger, and fall asleep. But perhaps—is this what the story is telling us?—perhaps it is not a simple thing to faithfully follow one's fate. Nor is it really a simple fate to carry such a wealth of graces and to fall asleep for a hundred years. These two elements in the story, the unparallelled beauty and the long deep sleep, are what light up the mind and set one questioning. One thing is certain. She is not merely a pretty girl waiting, after an eon of dreams, to be wakened by a lover. That she is a symbol, the core and heart of the world she inhabits, is shown by the fact, clearly stated in "The Petrified Mansion," "The Queen of Tubber Tintye," "The Sleeping Beauty in the Wood," and "*Dornroschen*," that when she sleeps, all about her sleep, when she wakens, her world wakes with her. One is reminded of the Grail Legend where, when the Fisher King is ill, his whole court is out of health and the countryside laid waste; when the King recovers, the courtiers, too, are whole again and the land begins to blossom. And there is an echo of this in the Norse sagas. We are told that when Brynhild (herself one of the world's sleepers) "lifted her head and laughed the whole castle dinned."

A symbol indeed. But what does it mean? Who is she, this peerless beauty, this hidden sleeping figure that has kindled the imaginations of so many generations and for whom children go about on tiptoe lest she be too soon wakened?

There are those who see the tale exclusively as a nature myth, as the earth in spring, personified as a maiden, awaking from the long dark sleep of winter; or as a seed hidden deep in the earth until the kiss of the sun makes it send forth leaves. This is undoubtedly an aspect of the story. But a symbol, by the very fact of being a symbol, has not one sole and absolute meaning. It throws out light in every direction. Meaning comes pouring from it.

As well as being a nature myth, it is also possible that there are elements of a secret and forgotten ritual in the theme, reminders of initiation ceremonies where the neophyte dies—or sleeps—on one level and awakes on another, as chrysalis wakes into butterfly. Or again it may be that since all fairy tales hark back to myth we are present here at the death and resurrection of a goddess, of Persephone down in the underworld biding her time till she returns to earth.

We can but guess, for the fairy tales never explain. But we should not let ourselves be fooled by their apparent simplicity. It is their role to say much in little. And not to explain is to set up in the hearer or the reader an inner friction in which one question inevitably leads to another and the answers that come are never conclusions. They never exhaust the meaning.

The latest version of the story, true to the law of the fairy tale, makes no attempt to explain. One could call it perhaps a meditation, for it broods and ponders upon the theme, elaborating it here and there with no other thought than of bringing out what the writer feels to be further hidden meanings. For instance, the Beauty, who has never before been given a name, is here called Rose—having regard not only to the Grimms' *"Dornroschen"* but also to Robert Graves' Druidic language of the tress in *The White Goddess*, where he speaks of the "erotic" briar. And further to underline this aspect, she is given a dove which in myth was sacred to Aphrodite, the Greek goddess of love; and a cat which was sacred to Freya, Aphrodite's Nordic counterpart. To these a lizard is added, not merely to provide the necessary fairy-tale third but to be assimilated to the symbol of the spindle which is nothing if not erotic.

All the known versions of the story have in them this strong element of eroticism. Indeed, it can be said with truth that every fairy tale that deals with a beautiful heroine and a lordly hero is, among many other things, speaking to us of love, laying down patterns and examples for all our human loving.

"The Sleeping Beauty," therefore, is not alone in this. What makes it unique is the spell of sleep. Brooding upon this, the why and the wherefore, we become, like the Sultana of the present version, full of wonder at her daughter's story. For inevitably, if the fairy-tale characters are our prototypes—which is what they are designed to be—we come to the point where we are forced to relate the stories and their meanings to ourselves. No amount of rationalising will bring us to the heart of the fairy tale. To enter it one must be prepared to let the rational reason go. The stories have to be loved for themselves before they will release their secrets. So, face to face with the Sleeping Beauty—who has long been the dream of every man and the hope of every woman—we find ourselves compelled to ask: what is it in *us* that at a certain moment suddenly falls asleep? Who lies hidden deep within us? And who will come at last to wake us, what aspect of ourselves?

Are we dealing here with the sleeping soul and all the external affairs of life that hem it in and hide it; something that falls asleep after childhood, something that not to waken would make life meaningless? To give an answer, supposing we had it, would be breaking the law of the fairy tale. And perhaps no answer is necessary. It is enough that we ponder upon and love the story and ask ourselves the question.

Part Two

Dornröschen

(BRIAR-ROSE)

A long time ago there were a King and a Queen who said every day, "Ah, if only we had a child!" But they never had one. But it happened that once when the Queen was bathing, a frog crept out of the water onto the land and said to her, "Your wish shall be fulfilled; before a year has gone by you shall have a daughter."

What the frog had said came true, and the Queen had a little girl who was so pretty that the King could not contain himself for joy, and ordered a great feast. He invited not only his kindred, friends, and acquaintances, but also the Wise Women, in order that they might be kind and well-disposed towards the child. There were thirteen of them in his kingdom, but, as he had only twelve golden places for them to eat out of, one of them had to be left at home.

The feast was held with all manner of splendour and when it came to an end the Wise Women bestowed their magic gifts upon the baby; one gave virtue, another beauty, a third riches, and so on with everything in the world that one can wish for.

When eleven of them had made their promises, suddenly the thirteenth came in. She wished to avenge herself for not having been invited and without greeting, or even looking at any one, she cried with a loud voice, "The King's daughter shall in her fifteenth year prick herself with a spindle and fall down dead." And, without saying a word more, she turned round and left the room.

They were all shocked; but the twelfth, whose good wish still remained unspoken, came forward, and as she could not undo the evil sentence but only soften it, she said, "It shall not be death, but a deep sleep of a hundred years, into which the Princess shall fall."

The King, who would fain keep his dear child from the misfortune, gave orders that every spindle in the whole kingdom should be burnt. Meanwhile, the gifts of the Wise Women were plenteously fulfilled in the young girl, for she was so beautiful, modest, good-natured, and wise, that everyone who saw her was bound to love her.

It happened that on the very day when she was fifteen years old, the King and the Queen were not at home, and the maiden was left in the palace quite alone. So she went round into all sorts of places, looked into rooms and bedchambers just as she liked, and at last came to an old tower. She climbed up the narrow winding-staircase and reached a little door. A rusty key was in the lock and when she turned it the door sprang open, and there in a little room sat an old woman with a spindle, busily spinning her flax.

"Good day, old dame" said the King's daughter, "what are you doing there?" "I am spinning," said the old woman and nodded her head. "What sort of thing is that, that rattles round so merrily?" said the girl, and she took the spindle and wanted to spin, too. But scarcely had she touched the spindle when the magic decree was fulfilled, and she pricked her finger with it.

And in the very moment when she felt the prick, she fell down upon the bed that stood there, and lay in a deep sleep. And this sleep extended over the whole palace; the King and Queen who had just come home, and had entered the great hall, began to go to sleep, and the whole of the court with them. The horses, too, went to sleep in the stable, the dogs in the yard, the pigeons upon the roof, the flies on the wall; even the fire that was flaming on the hearth became quiet and slept, the roast meat left off frizzling, and the cook, who was just going to pull the hair of the scullery boy, because he had forgotten something, let him go and went to sleep. And the wind fell, and on the trees before the castle not a leaf moved again.

But round about the castle there began to grow a hedge of thorns, which every year became higher, and at last grew close up round the castle and all over it, so that there was nothing of it to be seen, not even the flag upon the roof. But the story of the beautiful sleeping "Briar-Rose," for so the Princess was named, went about the country, so that from time to time Kings' sons came and tried to get through the thorny hedge into the castle.

But they found it impossible, for the thorns held fast together, as if they had hands, and the youths were caught in them, could not get loose again and died a miserable death.

After long, long years a King's son came again to that country, and heard an old man talking about the thorn hedge and that a castle was said to stand behind it in which a wonderfully beautiful princess, named Briar-Rose, had been asleep for a hundred years; and that the King and the Queen and the whole court were asleep likewise. He had heard, too, from his grandfather, that many King's sons had already come, and had tried to get through the thorny hedge, but they had remained sticking fast in it and had died a pitiful death. Then the youth said, "I am not afraid, I will go and see the beautiful Briar-Rose." The good old man might dissuade him as he would, he did not listen to his words.

But by this time the hundred years had just passed, and the day had come when Briar-Rose was to awake again. When the King's son came near to the thorn hedge, it was nothing but large and beautiful flowers, which parted from each other of their own accord, and let him pass unhurt, then they closed again behind him like a hedge. In the castle yard he saw the horses and the spotted hounds lying asleep; on the roof sat the pigeons with their heads under their wings. And when he entered the house, the flies were asleep upon the wall, the cook in the kitchen was still holding out his hand to seize the boy, and the maid was sitting by the black hen which she was going to pluck.

He went on farther, and in the great hall he saw the whole of the court lying asleep, and up by the throne lay the King and Queen.

Then he went on still farther, and all was so quiet that a breath could be heard, and at last he came to the tower, and opened the door into the little room where Briar-Rose was sleeping. There she lay, so beautiful that he could not turn his eyes away; and he stooped down and gave her a kiss. But as soon as he kissed her Briar-Rose opened her eyes and awoke and looked at him quite sweetly.

Then they went down together, and the King awoke and the Queen and the whole court and they all looked at each other in great astonishment. And the horses in the courtyard stood up and shook themselves; the hounds jumped up and wagged their tails; the pigeons upon the roof pulled out their heads from under their wings, looked around and flew into open country; the flies on the wall crept again; the fire in the kitchen burned up and flickered and cooked the meat; the joint began to turn and frizzle again, and the cook gave the boy such a box on the ear that he screamed and the maid plucked the fowl ready for the spit.

And then the marriage of the King's son with Briar-Rose was celebrated with all splendour and they lived contented to the end of their days.

—From *Grimm's Household Tales*,
Translated by Margaret Hunt

La Belle au Bois Dormant

(THE BEAUTY SLEEPING IN THE WOOD)

Once upon a time there were a king and a queen who were very unhappy because they had no children. They were more unhappy than words can tell. They went to all the watering places in the world. They tried everything—prayers, pilgrimages, vows to saints—but it made no difference. At last, however, the Queen conceived and gave birth to a daughter. A splendid christening was arranged. All the fairies who could be found in the country—there were seven of them—were invited to be godmothers, so that, if each of them brought a gift (as was the custom of the fairies in those days), the little Princess would be endowed with every quality imaginable.

When the christening was over, the whole company went back to the King's palace, where a great banquet had been prepared for the fairies. A magnificent place was laid for each of them, with a solid gold case containing a knife, a fork, and a spoon of finest gold inset with diamonds and

73

rubies. But just as they were all sitting down, who should come in but an old fairy who had not been invited because she had remained shut up in a tower for fifty years or more and everyone had believed her to be dead or under a spell.

The King ordered a place to be laid for her, but it was impossible to give her a gold case like the others because only seven had been made, for the seven known fairies. The old fairy took this as a slight and muttered threats under her breath. One of the younger fairies, who was sitting next to her, heard this muttering and guessed that she might give the Princess some harmful gift. So, the moment the meal was finished, she went and hid behind the tapestry. In that way she would be the last to speak and could make up, as far as lay in her power, for any harm that the old fairy might do.

Meanwhile, the fairies began to present their gifts to the Princess. The youngest gave her the gift of perfect beauty; the next promised that she should be marvellously witty and gay; the third that she should be exquisitely graceful in all her movements; the fourth, that she should dance beautifully; the fifth that she should sing like a nightingale; and the sixth that she should play all kinds of instruments to perfection. When the turn of the old fairy came, she said, trembling more with anger than with age, that the Princess would run a spindle into her hand and would die in consequence.

When they heard her make this terrible gift a shudder ran through the whole company, and none could restrain their tears. But at that moment the young fairy came out from behind the tapestry and said:

"Set your minds at rest, King and Queen, your daughter shall not die from this cause. It is true that I have not the power to undo entirely what my senior has done. The Princess *will* run a spindle into her hand. But, instead of

74

dying, she will simply fall into a deep sleep which will last a hundred years, at the end of which the son of a king will come to wake her."

Hoping to avoid the disaster predicted by the old fairy, the King immediately issued a proclamation forbidding all his subjects to spin with spindles, or to have spindles in their homes, on pain of death.

Fifteen or sixteen years later, when the King and Queen were away at one of their country houses, it happened that the young Princess was playing about in the castle. Running from room to room, she reached the top of a big tower and came to a little attic where a dear old woman was sitting by herself spinning. This old woman had not heard of the King's proclamation forbidding the use of spindles.

"What is that you are doing?" asked the Princess.

"Spinning, my dear," said the old woman, who did not know who she was.

"How pretty it is," said the Princess. "How do you do it? Give it to me and let me try."

No sooner had she taken it up than—since she was hasty and rather careless and, besides, the fairies had so ordained it—she ran the spindle into her hand and immediately fainted away.

The old woman was greatly upset and called for help. People came running from all over the palace. They poured water on the Princess's face, unlaced her dress, chafed her hands and rubbed her forehead with essence of rosemary, but nothing would bring her back to life.

Then the King, who had returned to the palace and came up to see what the noise was about, remembered the fairy's prophecy. Realising that this had to happen, since the fairies had said so, he had the Princess carried to the finest room in the palace and placed on a bed embroidered in gold and silver. She looked like an angel—she was so beautiful. Her swoon had not drained the colour from her face; her cheeks were still rosy, her lips like coral. Her eyes were closed, but she could be heard breathing gently, which showed that she was not dead.

The King gave orders that she was to be left to sleep there quietly until the day came when she was to awake. The good fairy who had saved her life by dooming her to sleep for a hundred years was in the Kingdom of Mataquin, twelve thousand leagues away, at the time of the accident. But the news was brought to her instantly by a little dwarf with seven-league boots (that is, boots which covered seven leagues at a single stride). The fairy set off immediately in a carriage of fire drawn by dragons, and was there within the hour. The King came out to hand her down from her carriage. She approved everything that he had done. But, as she was extremely farsighted, she reflected that, when the Princess eventually awoke, she would feel most uncomfortable to be all alone in that old castle. So this is what she did.

She touched with her wand everything in the castle, except the King and Queen; governesses, maids-of-honour, chambermaids, gentlemen-in-waiting, officers of the household, stewards, cooks, scullions, pot-boys, guards, doorkeepers, pages, footmen. She also touched all the horses in the stables, with the grooms, the big watchdogs, and little Puff, the Princess's puppy, who was lying beside her on the bed. No sooner had she touched them than they all fell asleep, to wake only when their mistress did, ready to serve her when she needed them. Even the roasting-spits which were turning before the fire crammed with partridges and pheasants went to sleep, and the fire also. All this was performed in a twinkling, for the fairies always did their work fast.

The King and Queen, having kissed their dear child

without her waking, left the castle and gave orders that no one was to go near it. These orders were not necessary for within a quarter of an hour there grew up all around such a number of big and little trees, brambles, and tangled thorns, that neither man nor beast could have passed through. Nothing but the tops of the towers could be seen and then only from a considerable distance. It was obvious that the fairy had worked another of her magic spells to guard the Princess from prying eyes while she slept.

At the end of a hundred years, the son of the King who was then reigning and who belonged to a different family from the sleeping Princess, was out hunting in that neighbourhood and inquired what were the towers which he could see above the trees of a thick wood.

His followers gave him different answers according to the versions they had heard. Some said that it was an old castle haunted by spirits; others that it was the place where all the witches of the region held their sabbath. The most widespread belief was that it was the home of an ogre who carried off all the children he could catch to eat them there undisturbed, since he alone had the power of passing through the wood.

The Prince did not know what to believe, when an old peasant came forward and said: "Your Highness, more than fifty years ago I heard my father say that there was a most beautiful princess in that castle. He said that she was to sleep for a hundred years and that she would be awakened by a king's son, for whom she was intended."

These words acted on the young Prince like a spur. He felt certain that this was an exploit which he could accomplish and, fired by love and the desire for glory, he determined to put the story to the test there and then. As he entered the wood, all the big trees, the brambles and the thorn bushes bent aside of their own accord to let him pass.

77

He advanced towards the castle, which he could see at the far end of a long avenue. He was a little surprised to find that none of his men had been able to follow him, since the trees had sprung back as soon as he had passed through. But that did not deter him from going on. A prince is always brave when he is young and in love. He reached the great forecourt, where everything that met his eyes might well have stricken him with fear. There was a dreadful silence. The image of death was everywhere. The place was full of the prostrate bodies of men and animals, all apparently dead. But the Prince soon saw, by the red noses and ruddy cheeks of the doorkeepers, that they were only asleep; and their glasses, which still contained a few drops of wine, showed plainly enough that they had fallen asleep while drinking.

He went on into a big courtyard paved with marble, up a staircase and into the guardroom, where the guards were drawn up in two lines with their harquebusses on their shoulders, snoring away loudly. He passed through several rooms filled with ladies and gentlemen who were all asleep, some on their feet, others seated. At last he came to a room with golden panelling and saw on a bed, whose curtains were drawn aside, the loveliest sight he had ever seen; a princess of about fifteen or sixteen, whose radiant beauty seemed to glow with a kind of heavenly light. Trembling and wondering, he drew near and knelt down before her.

Then, as the spell had come to its end, the Princess awoke and, looking at him more tenderly than would seem proper for a first glance, "Is it you, my Prince?" she said. "You have been a long time coming."

Delighted by these words, and still more so by the tone in which they were uttered, the Prince hardly knew how to express his joy and gratitude. He swore that he loved her better than life itself. His speech was halting, but it pleased her all the more; for the less ready the tongue, the stronger the love. He was more confused than she was and it was scarcely surprising. She had had time to think out what she would say to him, for it seems very probable (though the story does not say so) that the good fairy had arranged for her long sleep to be filled with pleasant dreams. In short, they went on talking to each other for four hours, and still had not said half the things they wanted to say.

Meanwhile, the whole palace had awakened with the Princess. Each had gone about his duties and, since they were not all in love, they were dying of hunger. The lady-in-waiting, as famished as the others, grew impatient and loudly announced that dinner was ready. The Prince helped the Princess to get up. She was fully dressed in sumptuous clothes, and the Prince took good care not to tell her that she was turned out just like my grandmother, even to the high starched collar. She was no less beautiful for that.

They passed into a hall of mirrors, and there they supped, attended by the officers of the Princess's household. Violins and oboes played old but delightful airs, which had not been heard for nearly a hundred years. And after supper, without wasting time, the chaplain married them in the palace chapel and the lady-in-waiting drew the bed-curtains round them. They slept little. The Princess hardly needed to and the Prince had to leave her early in the morning to get back to the town, where his father would be growing anxious about him.

The Prince told him that he had lost his way while out hunting in the forest and had spent the night in a charcoal-burner's hut, where he had supped on black bread and cheese. The King was an easygoing man and believed him. But his mother was not entirely convinced and noticing that he went out hunting nearly every day and always had an excuse ready when he did not come home at night, she felt certain that he was engaged in some love affair. For he lived with the Princess for more than two years and they had two children. The first, a daughter, was called Dawn and the second, a son, was called Day because he looked even more beautiful than his sister.

Several times the Queen tried to make her son confide in her by saying to him that it was natural to take one's pleasures in life, but he never dared reveal his secret to her. Although he loved her, he feared her because she came of a family of ogres, and the King had only married her for the sake of her wealth. It was even whispered that she had ogreish appetites herself and that when she saw little children about she had the greatest difficulty in restraining herself from pouncing on them. That was why the Prince would not confide in her.

But when the King died, as he did after two years, and the Prince became the master, he announced his marriage publicly and went with great ceremony to fetch his wife, the Queen, from the castle. She was given a royal welcome when she drove into the capital seated between her two children.

Some time after that, the King went to war against his neighbour, the Emperor Cantalabutto. He left the kingdom in charge of the Queen Mother, bidding her to take the greatest care of his wife and children. He was to be away at the war for the whole summer. As soon as he had gone, the Queen Mother sent her daughter-in-law and the children to a country house in in the woods where she would be able to satisfy her horrible appetites more easily. She herself followed them a few days later, and one evening she said to her steward: "I wish to have little Dawn for my dinner tomorrow."

"But Your Majesty—" said the steward.

"It is my wish," said the Queen (and her voice was the

voice of an ogress who is craving for human flesh) "and I wish to have her served with mustard-and-onion sauce."

The miserable steward, realising that it was useless to trifle with an ogress, took his largest knife and went up to little Dawn's room. She was then four years old and she came skipping and laughing to fling her arms round his neck and asked him for sweets. Tears came into his eyes and the knife fell from his hand. He went out to the farmyard and killed a young lamb which he cooked with such a delicious sauce that his mistress declared she had never eaten anything so good. At the same time he took away little Dawn and gave her to his wife to hide in the cottage they had at the bottom of the farmyard.

A week later the wicked Queen said to the steward: "I wish to have little Day for my supper."

He made no reply, having decided to trick her in the same way as before. He went to fetch little Day and found him with a tiny foil in his hand, fencing with a pet monkey, though he was only three. He carried him down to his wife, to be hidden with little Dawn, and served instead a very tender young kid which the ogress found excellent.

So far, things had gone very well. But one evening the wicked Queen said to the steward: "I wish to have the Queen, served with the same sauce as her children."

When he heard this, the poor steward despaired of tricking her again. The young Queen was over twenty, without counting the hundred years during which she had been asleep. Her skin was a little tough, although it was smooth and white. Where would he find a skin as tough as that among the farmyard animals? Since his own life was at stake, he made up his mind to cut the Queen's throat and went up to her room intending to act quickly. Working himself into a fury, he burst into the room, knife in hand. But he did not want to take her unawares, so he told her

81

with great respect of the order he had received from the Queen Mother.

"Do your duty, then," she said, baring her throat to the knife. "Carry out the order you have been given. I shall see my children again, my poor children whom I loved so dearly!" For she believed them to be dead, since they had been taken away without a word of explanation.

"No, no, Your Majesty," replied the unhappy steward, completely won over, "you shall not die and you shall still see your dear children. But you shall see them in my house, where I have hidden them. And I will trick the Queen again, by giving her a young doe to eat in place of you."

He took her quickly to his house and, leaving her there to embrace her children, he set about preparing a doe which the Queen Mother ate for supper with as much relish as if it had been the young Queen herself. She was well pleased with her cruelty and she intended to tell the King, when he came back, that ravening wolves had devoured his wife and his two children.

One evening when she was prowling as usual about the yards and courtyards of the castle to see if she could smell out some young human flesh, she heard the voice of little Day in a ground-floor room. He was crying because he had been naughty and his mother was threatening to have him whipped. She also heard little Dawn, who was begging for her brother to be let off.

The ogress recognised the voices of the Queen and her children and was furious to find that she had been tricked. The next morning she called in a voice of thunder for a huge vat to be placed in the middle of the courtyard and filled with toads, vipers, adders, and other poisonous reptiles. Into this were to be cast the Queen and her children, with the steward, his wife, and his servant, who had all been led out on her order with their hands tied behind their backs.

La Belle au Bois Dormant

They were standing there and the executioners were preparing to cast them into the vat when the King, who was not expected back so soon, came riding into the courtyard. He had been travelling posthaste and, filled with amazement, he demanded to know the meaning of this horrible sight. No one dared to enlighten him, but the ogress, furious at the turn things had taken, flung herself headlong into the vat and was devoured in an instant by the foul creatures which she had placed there. The King could not help feeling sorry, for she was his mother. But he soon consoled himself with his beautiful wife and his children.

—From Charles Perrault's *Fairy Tales*,
Translated by Geoffrey Brereton

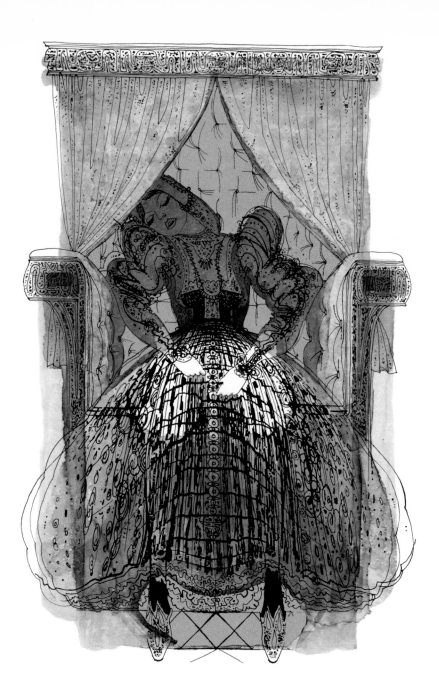

Sole, Luna, E Talia

(SUN, MOON, AND TALIA)

There was once a great king who, on the birth of his daughter—to whom he gave the name of Talia—commanded all the wise men and seers in the kingdom to come and tell him what her future would be. These wise men, after many consultations, came to the conclusion that she would be exposed to great danger from a small splinter in some flax. Thereupon the King, to prevent any unfortunate accident, commanded that no flax or hemp or any other similar material should ever come into his house.

One day when Talia was grown up she was standing by the window, and saw an old woman pass who was spinning. Talia had never seen a distaff and spindle, and therefore delighted with the dancing of the spindle. Prompted by curiosity, she had the old woman brought up to her, and taking the distaff in her hand, began to draw out the thread; but unfortunately a splinter in the hemp got under her fingernail, and she immediately fell dead upon the ground. At this terrible catastrophe the old woman fled from the room, rushing precipitously down the stairs. The stricken father, after having paid for this bucketful of sour wine with a barrelful of tears, left the dead Talia seated on a velvet chair under an embroidered canopy in the palace, which was in the middle of a wood. Then he locked the door and left forever the house which had brought him such evil fortune, so that he might entirely obliterate the memory of his sorrow and suffering.

It happened some time after that a falcon of a king who was out hunting in these parts flew in at the window of this house. As the bird did not return when called back, the King sent someone to knock at the door, thinking the house was inhabited. When they had knocked a long time in vain, the King sent for a vine-dresser's ladder, so that he might climb up himself and see what was inside. He climbed up and went in, and was astonished at not finding a living being anywhere. Finally he came to the room in which sat Talia as if under a spell.

The King called to her, thinking she was asleep; but since nothing he did or said brought her back to her senses, and being on fire with love, he carried her to a couch and, having gathered the fruits of love, left her lying there. Then he returned to his own kingdom and for a long time entirely forgot the affair.

Nine months later, Talia gave birth to two children, a boy and a girl, two splendid pearls. They were looked after by two fairies, who had appeared in the palace, and who put the babies to their mother's breast. Once, when one of the babies wanted to suck, it could not find the breast, but got into its mouth instead the finger that had been pricked. This the baby sucked so hard that it drew out the splinter, and Talia was roused as if from a deep sleep. When she saw the two jewels at her side, she clasped them to her breast and held them as dear as life; but she could not understand what had happened, and how she came to be alone in the palace with two children, having everything she required to eat brought to her without seeing anyone.

One day the King bethought himself of the adventure of the fair sleeper, and took the opportunity of another hunting expedition to go and see her. Finding her awake and with two prodigies of beauty, he was overpowered with joy. He told Talia what had happened and they made a great compact of friendship, and he remained several days in her company. Then he left her, promising to come again and take her back with him to his kingdom. When he reached his home he was forever talking of Talia and her children. At meals the names of Talia, Sun, and Moon (these were the children's names) were always on his lips; when he went to bed he was always calling one or the other.

The Queen had already had some glimmering of suspicion on account of her husband's long absence when hunting; and hearing his continued calling on Talia, Sun, and Moon, burned with a heat very different from the sun's heat, and calling the King's secretary, said to him: "Listen, my son, you are between Scylla and Charybdis, between the doorpost and the door, between the poker and the grate. If you tell me with whom it is that my husband is in love, I will make you rich; if you hide the truth from me, you shall never be found again, dead or alive." The man, on the one hand moved by fear and on the other egged on by interest, which is a bandage over the eyes of honour, a blinding of justice and a cast horseshoe to faith, told the Queen all, calling bread bread and wine wine.

Then she sent the same secretary in the King's name to tell Talia that he wished to see his children. Talia was delighted and sent the children. But the Queen, as soon as she had possession of them, with the heart of a Medea,

ordered the cook to cut their throats and to make them into
hashes and sauces and give them to their unfortunate
father to eat.

The cook, who was tender-hearted, was filled with pity
on seeing these two golden apples of beauty, and gave them
to his wife to hide and prepared two kids, making a
hundred different dishes of them. When the hour for
dinner arrived, the Queen had the dishes brought in, and
whilst the King was eating and enjoying them, exclaiming:
"How good this is, by the life of Lanfusa! How tasty this is,
by the soul of my grandmother!" she kept encouraging him,
saying: "Eat away, you are eating what is your own." The
first two or three times the King paid no attention to these
words, but as she kept up the same strain of music, he
answered: "I know very well I am eating what is my own;
you never brought anything into the house." And getting
up in a rage, he went off to a villa not far away to cool his
anger down.

The Queen, not satisfied with what she thought she
had already done, called the secretary again, and sent him
to fetch Talia herself, pretending that the King was expect-
ing her. Talia came at once, longing to see the light of her
eyes and little guessing that it was fire that awaited her.
She was brought before the Queen, who, with the face of a
Nero all inflamed with rage, said to her; "Welcome, Ma-
dame Troccola (busybody)! So you are the fine piece of
goods, the fine flower my husband is enjoying! You are the
cursed bitch that makes my head go round! Now you have
got into purgatory, and I will make you pay for all the harm
you have done me!"

Talia began to excuse herself, saying it was not her
fault and that the King had taken possession of her terri-
tory whilst she was sleeping. But the Queen would not
listen to her, and commanded that a great fire should be lit

in the courtyard of the palace and that Talia should be thrown into it.

The unfortunate Talia, seeing herself lost, threw herself on her knees before the Queen, and begged that at least she should be given time to take off the clothes she was wearing. The Queen, not out of pity for her, but because she wanted to save the clothes, which were embroidered with gold and pearls, said: "Undress—that I agree to."

Talia began to undress, and for each garment that she took off she uttered a shriek. She had taken off her dress, her skirt, and bodice and was about to take off her petticoat, and to utter her last cry, and they were just going to drag her away to reduce her to lye ashes, which they would throw into boiling water to wash Charon's breeches with, when the King saw the spectacle and rushed up to learn what was happening. He asked for his children, and heard from his wife, who reproached him for his betrayal of her, how she had made him eat them himself.

The King abandoned himself to despair. "What!" he cried, "am I the wolf of my own sheep? Alas, why did my veins not recognise the fountain of their own blood? You renegade Turk, this barbarous deed is the work of your hands? Go, you shall get what you deserve; there will be no need to send such a tyrant-faced one to the Colosseum to do penance!"

So saying, he ordered that the Queen should be thrown into the fire lighted for Talia, and that the secretary should be thrown in, too, for he had been her handle in this cruel game and the weaver of this wicked web. He would have had the same done to the cook who, as he thought, had cut up his children; but the cook threw himself at the King's feet, saying: "Indeed, my lord, for such a service there should be no other reward than a burning furnace; no pension but a spike-thrust from behind; no entertainment but that of being twisted and shrivelled in the fire; neither could there be any greater honour than for me, a cook, to have my ashes mingle with those of a queen. But this is not the thanks I expect for having saved your children from that spiteful dog who wished to kill them and return to your body what came from it."

The King was beside himself when he heard these words; it seemed to him as if he must be dreaming and that he could not believe his ears. Turning to the cook, he said: "If it is true that you have saved my children, you may be sure I will not leave you turning spits in the kitchen. You shall be in the kitchen of my heart, turning my will just as you please, and you shall have such rewards that you will account yourself the luckiest man in the world."

Whilst the King was speaking, the cook's wife, seeing her husband's difficulties, brought Sun and Moon up to their father, who, playing at the game of three with his wife and children, made a ring of kisses, kissing first one and then the other. He gave a handsome reward to the cook and made him Gentleman of the Bedchamber. Talia became his wife, and enjoyed a long life with her husband and children, finding it to be true that:

> *Lucky people, so tis said,*
> *Are blessed by Fortune whilst in bed.*

Translator's Note.
The sucking of a finger to obtain milk is found in many early Sanskrit works. A well-known example occurs in the *Mahabharata* where Mandhatr, who was born from his father's left side, was given Indra's finger to suck—with most surprising results, as far as his stature and strength were concerned.

There are also numerous folk tales in which the heart or other parts of the body of a relation or loved one are eaten by mistake, usually through revenge. [N.B. "The Juniper Tree"—TRANSLATOR]

There is a curious tale in Soma Deva (*Ocean of Story*, vol. 8, pp. 58 et. seq.) in which an ascetic lives with a nymph who subsequently becomes pregnant and gives birth to a child. The nymph is now forced to depart, but informs the ascetic that they can be united by his cooking and eating the baby. This he does with the desired result. Furthermore, Maruvhuti, the hero of the tale, eats two grains of rice from the dish and immediately acquires the power of spitting gold. Thus we see that the eating of human flesh is capable of producing supernatural powers—a theory far removed from being confined to folk tales.

—From *The Pentamerone of Giambattista Basile,* Translated from the Italian of Benedetto Groce by N. M. Penzer.

Editor's Note

There is a story in Campbell's *Popular Tales of the West Highlands* (Vol. 1, pp. 168–169) which resembles the present one as far as the connection between the hero and the sleeping girl is concerned, although all details are left to the reader's imagination. It is entitled "The Brown Bear of the Green Glen," and relates how John, the youngest son of a king in Erin, meets a woman, apparently asleep, in a little house. He kisses (?) her and departs and subsequently the girl gives birth to a child, to her great surprise. She is anxious to find out the identity of the father which she does by the help of a bird which settles on John's head.

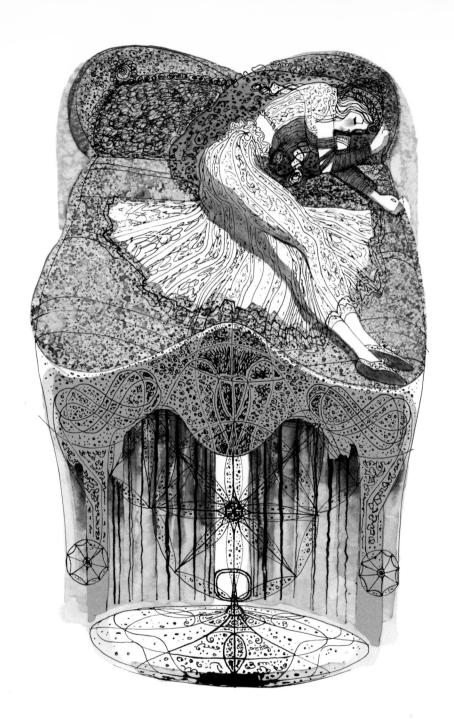

The Queen of Tubber Tintye

or (THE KING OF ERIN AND THE QUEEN OF THE LONESOME ISLAND)

There was a king in Erin long ago, and this king went out hunting one day, but saw nothing till near sunset, when what should come across him but a black pig.

"Since I've seen nothing all day but this black pig, I'll be at her now," said the king; so he put spurs to his horse and raced after the pig.

When the pig was on a hill he was in the valley behind her; when he was on a hill, the pig was in the valley before him. At last they came to the seaside, and the pig rushed out into the deep water straight from the shore. The king spurred on his horse and followed the black pig through the sea till his horse failed under him and was drowned.

Then the king swam on himself till he was growing weak, and said: "It was for the death of me that the black pig came in my way."

But he swam on some distance yet, till at last he saw land. The pig went up on an island; the king too went on shore, and said to himself: "Oh! it is for no good that I came here; there is neither house nor shelter to be seen." But he cheered up after a while, walked around, and said: "I'm a useless man if I can't find shelter in some place."

After going on a short space he saw a great castle in a valley before him. When he came to the front of the castle he saw that it had a low door with a broad threshold all covered with sharp-edged razors, and a low lintel of long-pointed needles. The path to the castle was covered with gravel of gold. The king came up, and went in with a jump over the razors and under the needles. When inside he saw a great fire on a broad hearth, and said to himself, "I'll sit down here, dry my clothes, and warm my body at this fire."

As he sat and warmed himself, a table came out before him with every sort of food and drink, without his seeing anyone bring it.

"Upon my honor and power," said the king of Erin, "there is nothing bad in this! I'll eat and drink my fill."

Then he fell to, and ate and drank his fill. When he had grown tired, he looked behind him, and if he did he saw a fine room, and in it a bed covered with gold. "Well," said he, "I'll go back and sleep in that bed a while, I'm so tired."

He stretched himself on the bed and fell asleep. In the night he woke up, and felt the presence of a woman in the room. He reached out his hand towards her and spoke, but got no answer; she was silent.

When morning came, and he made his way out of the castle, she spread a beautiful garden with her Druidic spells over the island—so great that though he travelled through it all day he could not escape from it. At sunset he was back at the door of the castle; and in he went over the razors and under the needles, sat at the fire, and the table came out before him as on the previous evening. He ate, drank, and slept on the bed; and when he woke in the night, there was the woman in the room; but she was silent and unseen as before.

When he went out on the second morning the king of Erin saw a garden three times more beautiful than the one of the day before. He travelled all day, but could not escape—could not get out of the garden. At sunset he was back at the door of the castle; in he went over the razors and under the needles, ate, drank, and slept, as before.

In the middle of the night he woke up, and felt the presence of the woman in the room. "Well," said he, "it is a wonderful thing for me to pass three nights in a room with a woman, and not see her nor know who she is!"

"You won't have that to say again, king of Erin," answered a voice. And that moment the room was filled with a bright light, and the king looked upon the finest woman he had ever seen. "Well, king of Erin, you are on Lonesome Island. I am the black pig that enticed you over the land and through the sea to this place, and I am queen of Lonesome Island. My two sisters and I are under a Druidic spell, and we cannot escape from this spell till your son and mine shall free us. Now, King of Erin, I will give you a boat tomorrow morning, and do you sail away to your own kingdom."

In the morning she went with him to the seashore to the boat. The king gave the prow of the boat to the sea, and its stern to the land; then he raised the sails, and went his way. The music he had was the roaring of the wind with the whistling of eels, and he broke neither oar nor mast till he landed under his own castle in Erin.

Three quarters of a year after, the queen of Lonesome Island gave birth to a son. She reared him with care from day to day and year to year till he was a splendid youth. She taught him the learning of wise men one half of the day, and warlike exercises with Druidic spells the other half.

One time the young man, the prince of Lonesome Island, came in from hunting, and found his mother sobbing and crying.

"Oh! what has happened to you, Mother?" he asked.

"My son, great grief has come to me. A friend of mine is going to be killed tomorrow."

"Who is he?"

"The king of Erin. The king of Spain has come against him with a great army. He wishes to sweep him and his men from the face of the earth, and take the kingdom himself."

"Well, what can we do? If I were there, I'd help the king of Erin."

"Since you say that, my son, I'll send you this very evening. With the power of my Druidic spells, you'll be in Erin in the morning."

The prince of Lonesome Island went away that night, and next morning at the rising of the sun he drew up his boat under the king's castle in Erin. He went ashore, and saw the whole land black with the forces of the king of Spain, who was getting ready to attack the king of Erin and sweep him and his men from the face of the earth.

The prince went straight to the king of Spain, and said, "I ask one day's truce."

"You shall have it, my champion," answered the king of Spain.

The prince then went to the castle of the king of Erin, and stayed there that day as a guest. Next morning early he dressed himself in his champion's array, and, taking his nine-edged sword, he went down alone to the king of Spain, and, standing before him, bade him guard himself.

They closed in conflict, the king of Spain with all his forces on one side, and the prince of Lonesome Island on the other. They fought an awful battle that day from sunrise till sunset. They made soft places hard, and hard places soft; they made high places low, and low places high; they brought water out of the center of hard gray rocks, and made dry rushes soft in the most distant parts of

Erin till sunset; and when the sun went down, the king of Spain and his last man were dead on the field.

Neither the king of Erin nor his forces took part in the battle. They had no need, and they had no chance.

Now the king of Erin had two sons, who were such cowards that they hid themselves from fright during the battle; but their mother told the king of Erin that her elder son was the man who had destroyed the king of Spain and all his men.

There was great rejoicing and a feast at the castle of the king of Erin. At the end of the feast the queen said: "I wish to give the last cup to this stranger who is here as a guest;" and taking him to an adjoining chamber which had a window right over the sea, she seated him in the open window and gave him a cup of drowsiness to drink. When he had emptied the cup and closed his eyes, she pushed him out into the darkness.

The prince of Lonesome Island swam on the water for four days and nights, till he came to a rock in the ocean, and there he lived for three months, eating the seaweeds of the rock, till one foggy day a vessel came near and the captain cried out: "We shall be wrecked on this rock!" Then he said, "There is someone on the rock; go and see who it is."

They landed, and found the prince, his clothes all gone, his body black from the seaweed, which was growing all over it.

"Who are you?" asked the captain.

"Give me first to eat and drink. Then I'll talk," said he.

They brought him food and drink; and when he had eaten and drunk, the prince said to the captain: "What part of the world have you come from?"

"I have just sailed from Lonesome Island," said the captain. "I was obliged to sail away, for fire was coming from every side to burn my ship."

"Would you like to go back?"

"I should indeed."

"Well, turn around; you'll have no trouble if I am with you."

The captain returned. The queen of Lonesome Island was standing on the shore as the ship came in.

"Oh, my child!" cried she. "Why have you been away so long?"

"The queen of Erin threw me into the sea after I had kept the head of the king of Erin on him, and saved her life too."

"Well, my son, that will come up against the queen of Erin on another day."

Now, the prince lived on Lonesome Island three years longer, till one time he came home from hunting, and found his mother wringing her hands and shedding bitter tears.

"Oh! what has happened?" asked he.

"I am weeping because the king of Spain has gone to take vengeance on the king of Erin for the death of his father, whom you killed."

"Well, Mother, I'll go to help the king of Erin, if you give me leave."

"Since you have said it, you shall go this very night."

He went to the shore. Putting the prow of his bark to the sea and her stern to land, he raised high the sails, and heard no sound as he went but the pleasant wind and the whistling of eels, till he pulled up his boat next morning under the castle of the king of Erin and went on shore.

The whole country was black with the troops of the king of Spain, who was just ready to attack, when the prince stood before him, and asked a truce till next morning.

"That you shall have, my champion," answered the king. So there was peace for that day.

Next morning at sunrise, the prince faced the king of Spain and his army, and there followed a struggle more terrible than that with his father; but at sunset neither the king of Spain nor one of his men was left alive.

The two sons of the king of Erin were frightened almost to death, and hid during the battle, so that no one saw them or knew where they were. But when the king of Spain and his army were destroyed, the queen said to the king: "My elder son has saved us." Then she went to bed, and taking the blood of a chicken in her mouth, spat it out, saying: "This is my heart's blood; and nothing can cure me now but three bottles of water from Tubber Tintye, the flaming well."

When the prince was told of the sickness of the queen of Erin, he came to her and said: "I'll go for the water if your two sons will go with me."

"They shall go," said the queen; and away went the three young men toward the East, in search of the flaming well.

In the morning they came to a house on the roadside; and going in, they saw a woman who had washed herself in a golden basin which stood before her. She was then wetting her head with the water in the basin, and combing her hair with a golden comb. She threw back her hair, and looking at the prince, said: "You are welcome, sister's son. What is on you? Is it the misfortune of the world that has brought you here?"

"It is not; I am going to Tubber Tintye for three bottles of water."

"That is what you'll never do; no man can cross the fiery river or go through the enchantments around Tubber Tintye. Stay here with me, and I'll give you all I have."

"No, I cannot stay, I must go on."

"Well, you'll be in your other aunt's house tomorrow night, and she will tell you all."

Next morning, when they were getting ready to take the road, the elder son of the queen of Erin was frightened at what he had heard, and said: "I am sick; I cannot go farther."

"Stop here where you are till I come back," said the prince. Then he went on with the younger brother, till at sunset they came to a house where they saw a woman wetting her head from a golden basin, and combing her hair with a golden comb. She threw back her hair, looked at the prince, and said: "You are welcome, sister's son! What brought you to this place? Was it the misfortune of the world that brought you to live under Druidic spells like me and my sisters?" This was the elder sister of the queen of the Lonesome Island.

"No," said the prince, "I am going to Tubber Tintye for three bottles of water from the flaming well."

"Oh, sister's son, it's a hard journey you're on! But stay here tonight; tomorrow morning I'll tell you all."

In the morning the prince's aunt said: "The queen of the Island of Tubber Tintye has an enormous castle, in which she lives. She has a countless army of giants, beasts, and monsters to guard the castle and the flaming well. There are thousands upon thousands of them, of every form and size. When they get drowsy, and sleep comes on them, they sleep for seven years without waking. The queen has twelve attendant maidens, who live in twelve chambers. She is in the thirteenth and innermost chamber herself. The queen and the maidens sleep during the same seven years as the giants and beasts. When the seven years are over, they all wake up, and none of them sleep again for seven other years. If any man could enter the castle during the seven years of sleep, he could do what he liked. But the island on which the castle stands is girt by a river of fire and surrounded by a belt of poison trees."

The aunt now blew on a horn, and all the birds of the air gathered around her from every place under the heavens, and she asked each in turn where it dwelt, and each told her; but none knew of the flaming well, till an old eagle said: "I left Tubber Tintye today."

"How are all the people there?" asked the aunt.

"They are all asleep since yesterday morning," answered the old eagle.

The aunt dismissed the birds; and turning to the prince, said, "Here is a bridle for you. Go to the stables, shake the bridle, and put it on whatever horse runs out to meet you."

Now the second son of the queen of Erin said: "I am too sick to go farther."

"Well, stay here till I come back," said the prince, who took the bridle and went out.

The prince of the Lonesome Island stood in front of his aunt's stables, shook the bridle, and out came a dirty, lean little shaggy horse.

"Sit on my back, son of the king of Erin and the queen of Lonesome Island," said the little shaggy horse.

This was the first the prince had heard of his father. He had often wondered who he might be, but had never heard who he was before.

He mounted the horse, which said: "Keep a firm grip now, for I shall clear the river of fire at a single bound, and pass the poison trees; but if you touch any part of the trees, even with a thread of the clothing that's on you, you'll never eat another bite; and as I rush by the end of the castle of Tubber Tintye with the speed of the wind, you must spring from my back through an open window that is there; and if you don't get in at the window, you're done for. I'll wait for you outside till you are ready to go back to Erin."

The prince did as the little horse told him. They crossed the river of fire, escaped the touch of the poison trees, and as the horse shot past the castle, the prince sprang through the open window, and came down safe and sound inside.

The whole place, enormous in extent, was filled with sleeping giants and monsters of sea and land—great whales, long slippery eels, bears, and beasts of every form and kind. The prince passed through them and over them till he came to a great stairway. At the head of the stairway he went into a chamber, where he found the most beautiful woman he had ever seen, stretched on a couch asleep. "I'll have nothing to say to you," thought he, and went on to the next; and so he looked into twelve chambers. In each was a woman more beautiful than the one before. But when he reached the thirteenth chamber and opened the door, the flash of gold took the sight from his eyes. He stood a while till the sight came back, and then entered. In the great bright chamber was a golden couch, resting on wheels of gold. The wheels turned continually; the couch went round and round, never stopping night or day. On the couch lay the queen of Tubber Tintye; and if her twelve maidens were beautiful, they would not be beautiful if seen near her. At the foot of the couch was Tubber Tintye itself—the well of fire. There was a golden cover upon the well, and it went round continually with the couch of the queen.

"Upon my word," said the prince, "I'll rest here a while." And he went up on the couch, and never left it for six days and nights.

On the seventh morning he said, "It is time for me now to leave this place." So he came down and filled the three bottles with water from the flaming well. In the golden chamber was a table of gold, and on the table a leg of mutton with a loaf of bread; and if all the men in Erin were to eat for a twelvemonth from the table, the mutton and the bread would be in the same form after the eating as before.

The prince sat down, ate his fill of the loaf and the leg of mutton, and left them as he had found them. Then he rose up, took his three bottles, put them in his wallet, and was leaving the chamber, when he said to himself: "It would be a shame to go away without leaving something by which the queen may know who was here while she slept." So he wrote a letter, saying that the son of the king of Erin and the queen of the Lonesome Island had spent six days and nights in the golden chamber of Tubber Tintye, had taken away three bottles of water from the flaming well, and had eaten from the table of gold. Putting this letter under the pillow of the queen, he went out, stood in the open window, sprang on the back of the lean and shaggy little horse, and passed the trees and river unharmed.

When they were near his aunt's house, the horse stopped, and said: "Put your hand into my ear, and draw out of it a Druidic rod; then cut me into four quarters, and strike each quarter with the rod. Each one of them will become the son of a king, for four princes were enchanted and turned into the lean little shaggy horse that carried you to Tubber Tintye. When you have freed the four princes from this form you can free your two aunts from the spell that is on them, and take them with you to Lonesome Island."

The prince did as the horse desired; and straightway four princes stood before him, and thanking him for what he had done, they departed at once, each to his own kingdom.

The prince removed the spell from his aunts, and, travelling with them and the two sons of the queen of Erin, all soon appeared at the castle of the king.

When they were near the door of their mother's chamber, the elder of the two sons of the queen of Erin stepped up to the prince of Lonesome Island, snatched the three bottles from the wallet that he had at his side, and running up to his mother's bed, said: "Here, Mother, are the three bottles of water which I brought you from Tubber Tintye."

"Thank you, my son; you have saved my life," said she.

The prince went on his bark and sailed away with his aunts to Lonesome Island, where he lived with his mother seven years.

When seven years were over, the queen of Tubber Tintye awoke from her sleep in the golden chamber; and with her the twelve maidens and all the giants, beasts, and monsters that slept in the great castle.

When the queen opened her eyes, she saw a boy about six years old playing by himself on the floor. He was very beautiful and bright, and he had gold on his forehead and silver on his poll. When she saw the child, she began to cry and wring her hands, and said: "Some man has been here while I slept."

Straightway she sent for her Seandallglic (old blind sage), told him about the child, and asked: "What am I to do now?"

The old blind sage thought a while, and then said: "Whoever was here must be a hero; for the child has gold on his forehead and silver on his poll, and he never went from this place without leaving his name behind him. Let search be made, and we shall know who he was."

Search was made, and at last they found the letter of the prince under the pillow of the couch. The queen was now glad, and proud of the child.

Next day she assembled all her forces, her giants and guards; and when she had them drawn up in line, the army was seven miles long from van to rear. The queen opened through the river of fire a safe way for the host, and led it on till she came to the castle of the king of Erin. She held all the land near the castle, so the king had the sea on one side, and the army of the queen of Tubber Tintye on the other, ready to destroy him and all that he had. The queen sent a herald for the king to come down.

"What are you going to do?" asked the king when he came to her tent. "I have had trouble enough in my life already, without having more of it now."

"Find for me," said the queen, "the man who came to my castle and entered the golden chamber of Tubber Tintye while I slept, or I'll sweep you and all you have from the face of the earth."

The king of Erin called down his elder son, and asked: "Did you enter the chamber of the queen of Tubber Tintye?"

"I did."

"Go, then, and tell her so, and save us."

He went; and when he told the queen, she said: "If you entered my chamber, then mount my gray steed."

He mounted the steed; and if he did, the steed rose in the air with a bound, hurled him off his back, in a moment, threw him on a rock, and dashed the brains out of his head.

The king called down his second son, who said that he had been in the golden chamber. Then he mounted the gray steed, which killed him as it had his brother.

Now the queen called the king again, and said: "Unless you bring the man who entered my golden chamber while I slept, I'll not leave a sign of you or anything you have upon the face of the earth."

Straightway the king sent a message to the queen of Lonesome Island, saying: "Come to me with your son and your two sisters!"

The queen set out next morning, and at sunset she drew up her boat under the castle of the king of Erin. Glad were they to see her at the castle, for great dread was on all.

Next morning the king went down to the queen of Tubber Tintye, who said: "Bring me the man who entered my castle, or I'll destroy you and all you have in Erin this day."

The king went up to the castle; immediately the prince of Lonesome Island went to the queen.

"Are you the man who entered my castle?" asked she.

"I don't know," said the prince.

"Go up now on my gray steed!" said the queen.

He sat on the gray steed, which rose under him into the sky. The prince stood on the back of the horse, and cut three times with his sword as he went up under the sun. When he came to the earth again, the queen of Tubber Tintye ran over to him, put his head on her bosom, and said: "You are the man."

Now she called the queen of Erin to her tent, and drawing from her own pocket a belt of silk, slender as a cord, she said: "Put this on."

The queen of Erin put it on, and then the queen of Tubber Tintye said: "Tighten, belt!" The belt tightened till the queen of Erin screamed with pain. "Now tell me," said the queen of Tubber Tintye, "who was the father of your elder son."

"The gardener," said the queen of Erin.

Again the queen of Tubber Tintye said: "Tighten, belt!" The queen of Erin screamed worse than before; and she had good reason, for she was cut nearly in two. "Now tell me who was the father of your second son."

"The big brewer," said the queen of Erin.

Said the queen of Tubber Tintye to the king of Erin: "Get this woman dead."

The king put down a big fire then, and when it was blazing high, he threw the wife in, and she was destroyed at once.

"Now do you marry the queen of Lonesome Island, and my child will be grandchild to you and to her," said the queen of Tubber Tintye.

This was done, and the queen of Lonesome Island became queen of Erin and lived in the castle by the sea. And the queen of Tubber Tintye married the prince of Lonesome Island, the champion who entered the golden chamber while she slept.

Now the king of Erin sent ten ships with messages to all the kings of the world, inviting them to come to the wedding of the queen of Tubber Tintye and his son, and to his own wedding with the queen of Lonesome Island.

The queen removed the Druidic spells from her giants, beasts, and monsters; then went home, and made the prince of Lonesome Island king of Tubber Tintye and lord of the golden chamber.

—From *Myths and Folk-lore of Ireland*,
retold by Jeremiah Curtin

The Petrified Mansion

Once upon a time there was a prince who set out on his travels into foreign countries, alone, without taking with him any valuables. His sword was his only companion. He crossed mountains, seas, rivers, and at length came to a grand mansion. He entered it; and great was his surprise to find petrified forms of men and animals in all the apartments through which he passed. Even the weapons in the armoury were not exceptions. There was in one of the halls a stone statue dressed in royal splendour, surrounded by other statues gorgeously equipped. The lonely house greatly frightened the prince, but just as he was on the point of quitting it he reached the presence of a very beautiful damsel reposing on a *khat* (bed) of gold, and surrounded by lotuses of the same metal. She lay quite motionless and was apparently dead. There was not the softest breath perceptible in her. The prince was enamoured of her beauty and sat with his eyes fixed upon her. But one day he happened to notice a stick of gold near the girl's pillow. He took it up, and was turning it round and round for inspection, when it suddenly touched her forehead; and instantly she started up, fully conscious. The whole house resounded with the clamour of human tongues, the clanking of arms, the songs of birds, and the sounds of domestic animals. It was full of life and joy. Heralds made proclamations, ministers speechified in the courtroom, and the king engaged himself in the discharge of his royal duties.

The prince was struck speechless with wonder; and the princess was equally astonished. The servants entered the room, and finding a princelike youth seated by their master's daughter, hastened to the king with the intelligence. He hurried to the spot, and seeing the prince, asked him who he was. The prince told him; and the royal family, with all the other inmates of the palace, acclaimed him as their deliverer. They said that the touch of a silver stick had petrified them all, and that their revival was the result of his having touched the princess with the stick of gold. In recognition of the very great service he had rendered them, the prince was rewarded with the princess's hand; and great were the rejoicings on the joyous occasion.

Meanwhile in his own home his parents mourned for the prince as the years passed and he did not return. The queen had taken to her bed, and the king had become blind with weeping. They were disconsolate, and courted death as the only termination of their great grief. The whole kingdom was overcast with sadness, which was, however, ultimately removed when one day the long-lost prince appeared with his bride. Joyous acclamations rent the air; and the royal couple, being informed of the return of their dear son, hastened out to the gate and embraced him and the princess. At the touch of the stick of gold the king regained his sight, and the queen her health, and they lived for years in the enjoyment of great happiness. At length, leaving the throne to his son, the king with the queen retired to spend a secluded and godly life in the depths of the forest.

—From *Bengal Fairy Tales*, by F. B. Bradley-Birt.